A Better Place

Other Writing by K.J. Stevens

    Introspection—a collection of poetry

    Corvallis Road—short stories written with Travis Mulhauser

    A Rainy Day—a quarterly prose newsletter

    HOPE at **www.kjstevens.20m.com**—stories, poetry and prose

Stories and poetry have also been published by:

    Sabine

    The Open Scroll

    TheWriteGallery

    The Oak

    The Alpena News

    Framework

    Prose Ax

    Comrades

    Events Quarterly

    Sulisa

    Ephiphany

    The Next Voice You Hear

A Better Place

A collection of short stories. A work of fiction.

Written by K.J. Stevens

Writer's Showcase
San Jose New York Lincoln Shanghai

A Better Place

All Rights Reserved © 2002 by Kim L. Stevens Jr.

No part of this book may be reproduced or transmitted in any form or by any means, graphic, electronic, or mechanical, including photocopying, recording, taping, or by any information storage retrieval system, without the permission in writing from the publisher.

Writer's Showcase
an imprint of iUniverse, Inc.

For information address:
iUniverse, Inc.
5220 S. 16th St., Suite 200
Lincoln, NE 68512
www.iuniverse.com

Cover art Copyright 2002 by Rita Stevens.

ISBN: 0-595-22424-5

Printed in the United States of America

✶✶✶✶✶✶

to my Family

Mom & Dad, Kevin & Christy, Keith & Melanie

and to Steph, for Everything.

✶✶✶✶✶✶

Contents

Jesus and Terry Bradshaw..1
Another Sunday..9
Fishing..17
Merry Christmas...23
An Accident...29
The Horn...35
Yellow..51
Driving in the Rain...61
Flag Day...73
The Drive..83
A Better Place...95

Jesus and Terry Bradshaw

*A*bigail Johnson lived in a huge house next door. It was baby blue with sweeping ornamental eves and pink shutters. A dollhouse. Her dad was a Vietnam veteran turned Chrysler executive and traveled a lot. Sometimes when he was home on weekends, I'd see him outside spraying around the foundation of their house with weed and insect killers. One weekend when Abigail was staying at a girlfriend's house, I walked over to talk to Mr. Johnson.

"I don't like bugs," he said.

I sat down on the front steps and watched him spray the ground with white foamy liquid.

"I like dragonflies," I said.

He stopped spraying.

"Why dragonflies?"

"Because they like people. Ever have one sit on your shoulder or something?"

"Yeah and I've killed them all!" Mr. Johnson said, spraying again.

"Dragonflies are good. If you catch one, you'll be married within a year."

Mr. Johnson set the spraying apparatus down and stood in front of me. His thick, black hair was wetted with perspiration. His powder blue golf shirt was tucked into a pair of black sweat pants.

"Where did you hear that?"

"It's an old superstition," I said. "I'm surprised you haven't heard it."

"I have and it's another reason I hate bugs."

Mr. Johnson sat down and took off his shoes. He wasn't wearing any socks. His toes were long and skinny, like fingers. A centipede crept along between his feet as he looked at the sky and rubbed his toes in the grass.

"Getting married's a good thing, isn't it?" I asked.

Mr. Johnson looked over his shoulder at the house.

"Listen, son. Getting married isn't decided by a bug."

"How do you know?"

"Why are you so concerned with bugs and marriage?"

"I'm not. I just like dragonflies, I guess."

"I've seen bugs that could carry you away and eat you alive."

Mr. Johnson put his shoes back on and turned to spraying again. I went inside to talk to Mrs. Johnson.

Abigail's ex-hippie mom was an art instructor at St. Anne's. When she wasn't teaching, she was organizing rummage sales or car washes and the outings these activities funded. Hiking and camping on Beaver Island, or trips downstate to the Detroit Zoo. When I walked into the house she was sitting in the livingroom, drawing a picture of a tree.

"Nice willow tree." I said.

"How do you know it's a willow?"

"We studied trees last year in sixth grade. Willows were on the list."

"I like willows," she said. "I wish we had more around here. They bring good luck."

Mrs. Johnson was chewing gum with her mouth wide open. She smelled good, like cinnamon, but the sound of her, all tongue and saliva was sickening.

"What are you drawing it for?"

"It's going to be used as a design for fund-raiser tickets."

"Where are you headed now?"

Mrs. Johnson stopped drawing. She turned to look at me. Her glasses were riding low on her freckled nose. A long strand of her strawberry-blonde hair hung down between her green eyes. Her tan blouse was open three buttons down. She looked nice.

"I'm planning to take the youth group to Willow Park."

"In Rogers City?" I asked.

She moved closer to me. She was still chewing that gum. It was red gum. I could see it rolling around in her mouth.

"Would you like to go?" she asked.

I backed away from her.

"I don't know."

"It'd be nice if you went because then I *know* Abigail would go."

"When's she coming home anyway?"

Mrs. Johnson stood up then brushed by me.

"She'll be home this evening. Her grandma's funeral is tomorrow." She walked into the kitchen. "Would you like some Tang?"

I didn't like Tang and although Mrs. Johnson looked nice, her chewing was driving me bonkers.

"No thanks. I'm gonna head home."

I figured it was better not to stick around. Her mentioning the funeral made me sad and I didn't feel like getting talked into going to Willow Park in Rogers City.

Mrs. Johnson took the Tang out of the cupboard and went to making herself some, anyway.

"Alright then. I'll tell Abigail you stopped by."

When I went outside Mr. Johnson was at the end of the driveway talking to the mailman. I waved to them then trotted down the path toward home. Grasshoppers jumped along ahead of me. Big gray ones were buzzing up from the tall grass alongside the path flying five to ten yards at a time. I imagined that beneath the grass, and maybe even deep in the soil, bugs of all kinds were creeping, crawling, and hopping their way to my yard, trying to escape Mr. Johnson and his foam.

It was early Sunday afternoon when Abigail came to my door. She had just come from the funeral and it was the first time I'd ever seen her in a dress. It was knee-high, sleeveless, and light blue. Her blonde hair was pulled into long pigtails and her fingernails were bright red. Her eyes were colored with mascara and her lips were pink. She didn't look anything like the Abigail Johnson I played with everyday. The Abigail that hid away in the bushes with me trading football cards. The girl who wore jeans and Pittsburgh Steeler jerseys.

"Wanna do something?" she asked.

"You look different."

Abigail looked herself over.

"Yeah well, do you wanna do something or not?"

I snatched two bottles of Mountain Dew from the refrigerator and went outside with her. The day was bright with sun. The south wind was warm and gusty. Little brown winged moths lined the trail as we walked. They were clumped together atop patches of white clover. Every third or fourth step, when Abigail reached down to pop the head of a Black-eyed Susan, the moths puffed into the sky.

The path was narrow, a rut worn into the ground, and Abigail's thin ankles wobbled in her light blue satiny shoes.

"Good walkin' shoes?" I asked.

She ignored me or was so caught up in the moths, or flowers, or her grandma, that she didn't hear me. When we reached her yard the wind came up and lifted the dress from her knees.

"I hate this dress!" She shouted.

Abigail held the fabric down against her thighs as we walked toward the bushes.

I handed her a pop then looked away from her to the lilacs in the yard. Sparrows and chickadees darted in and out of them and I could hear bees buzzing. We had a hide-out in the lilacs, an area where we had dragged in a table, two chairs and an ironing board. For decorations we had posters of Jesus and Terry Bradshaw nailed to the branches. We used an old Converse basketball shoe for our telephone and a cardboard box for our television.

Under the t.v. there were two ammunition boxes wrapped in plastic. One was mine and one was hers. They were packed full of football cards. She had the 1982 Pittsburgh Steelers set, complete with Terry Bradshaw—all long blond hair and blue collar grace. He was set in this great pose, cocked back to pass, forearm bursting with strength, and almost every day I tried to get it from her. Not because I wanted a Bradshaw card all that much, but because I wanted to see if she'd break the set.

Our entry into the bushes sent birds and bees flying. A chickadee zipped over our heads and landed on our t.v. It watched us a second or two, chirped, then left a white dropping before flying away. Abigail opened our sodas and cursed the birds under her breath. I got the ammo boxes out, unwrapped them, and started in on a deal.

"How bout I give you Joe Montana and Steve Deberg and you give me Terry Bradshaw?"

Abigail sipped her pop then walked over to the ironing board. She ironed a bit and thought. A bumble bee landed on the board next to her and she shooed it away.

"So? How bout it?" I asked.

The bee landed on the neck of my bottle, crawled to the lip and tried to get inside. I flicked it away with my finger. Abigail picked up the Converse telephone and spoke into the laces. She glanced at the television and talked to an imaginary pest control agency. She wanted to know how to eliminate unwanted birds and pesky bees. I thumbed through her Steeler set, waiting.

"Isn't your Mom gonna have a fit about you wearing that dress in here?"

She hung up the phone then walked over to me. She smelled fresh and sweet like Downy fabric softener and strawberries.

"She and Dad went back to the funeral home."

"I'm sorry about your Grandma," I said.

Abigail picked up the cards I offered to trade. She held them at arms length toward the sky to look them over. The underside of her arm was smooth and milky white. She put the cards down onto the table to examine them more closely. I stood and walked over to Jesus. His poster was hanging crooked. The bee was crawling over his face. I flicked it away then straightened the picture.
"I don't know about Joe Montana," She said, tapping his card with her new, bright red fingernails. "He looks a little small for the NFL."
"Abigail, he's the quarterback of the future!"
She walked over to Bradshaw's poster and kissed it.
"He's no Terry Bradshaw."
The bee zipped round her head and she swatted it. It hit the ground then buzzed back up and stung her on the cheek. My heart leapt.
"Holy smokes! You alright?"
Abigail ran out of the lilacs, her pigtails bouncing wildly. I followed her out, breathing deep, taking all of her in. Her dress swayed back and forth revealing skin I'd never even thought of before. When she got to the steps of her house she sat down and began to cry. I sat down beside her.
"Are you allergic?" I asked.
Abigail rubbed a tear away from the large welt forming under her eye. She was staring at the ground watching a dead cabbage moth being dragged away by an ant. I imagined Mr. Johnson would really be at it now. Spraying everything with spite.
"You look really pretty," I said.
Abigail looked at me. The summer sun had sprinkled freckles across her face. She smiled so I leaned into her and kissed her on the place where the bee had got her. She looked at the moth again and her smile faded. I stood up, but she pulled me back down and

hugged me. It was strong and hard and lived only a second. Just as quickly, she pulled away, stood up, and went inside.

I stepped away from her house and headed toward mine. I watched a sparrow flying over me toward my house. I wondered what it looked like from up there. I thought maybe the trail connecting our yards looked like a vein or a snake. I wondered if I looked small, like an ant, when I walked the trail. The sparrow dipped and bobbed its way into the white sun and I lost sight of it.

Another Sunday

Before Dad disappeared around back of the woodshed with the hatchet he told me to mind Grandpa and do as I was told if I wanted to go fishing. So it was a sticky hot Sunday afternoon and I was left on the steps of Grandpa's house waiting. Grandpa's black lab, Bo, was sitting beside me panting. He smelled like something dead and was nipping at the flies that buzzed around him.

The lilacs beside the deck were in bloom so I leaned over into them to breathe. A monarch butterfly fluttered out of the bushes and whirled round. It jetted up quickly, then descended in crazed, lazy loops. It landed on the ground below me near a dead sparrow. I watched two ants use a grassblade as a ramp and wander into the sparrow's beak. I stared at the bird, focusing with all my might, and wished it to flight until the sparrow's chest moved. One of the ants scurried out through an empty eye socket and disappeared into the grass. I waited for the other one, but it didn't come. The sparrow took another breath and I realized that maggots had become the bird's lungs.

The kitchen window rattled open above me. It was my Grandpa.

"Just foolin' with that stinkin' mutt again, hey?"

"I'm waiting for Dad, Gramp."

"Well wait in here, goddammit! I told him I'd keep an eye on ya and I can't be chasin' ya all over the goddamned yard!"

Since Grandpa was cursing, I knew he'd been drinking. And Bo seemed to know too because he stood, stretched, then sauntered away down the steps. A chorus of bulging green flies followed him as he sniffed his way to the sparrow and nosed it over. When his ears perked up with curiosity, I could see that where short, velvety black hair had been pink flesh now glistened. Flies had eaten his eartips raw. I thought I had read somewhere that putting Vaseline or Neosporin on a dog's ears would help prevent infection and keep the flies away, so I thought I'd ask if Grandpa had any.

I looked up at Grandpa. The sunshine was reflecting off his glasses. His eyes were silver-white discs. I couldn't tell how much he'd been drinking.

"Got any Vaseline?"

"What the hell for?"

I looked away from him and back to the ground. My eyesight was spotty. I closed my eyes.

"For Bo's ears. They're all ate up."

"Where in earth did ya learn that?"

"I read it somewhere."

"Read it! Why would ya wanna put goop all over his damned ears?"

I opened my eyes, the spots were still there.

"So he won't get an infection," I said.

"I tell ya who's gonna get an infection! You, if ya don't get your ass in here!"

I tried to focus on the shed, to where Dad had disappeared, but I still couldn't see.

"What have you got Dad doing back there, anyway?" I asked.

"Jackie, just git in here!"

And with that, Grandpa slammed the window shut.

I closed my eyes again and clenched the lids like tiny fists. When I opened them again, Bo, his flies, the sparrow, and the sunspots were gone. The sun was beating down, filling me with summer boredom and all I wanted was to go fishing as I gazed out over the lawn.

Two white moths were clinging to each other in midair. They danced a bit then went their separate ways. One ascended into the crisp blue sky, floating dizzily toward a long white vapor stream that a faraway plane had left behind. The other landed to rest awhile on Grandpa's shed. It was a homemade, leaning contraption and its roof had been blown away in an April storm. It was another thing Grandpa expected Dad to get done. And Dad came every Sunday with intentions of fixing it, but Grandpa always insisted that there were more important things that needed to be done. Today it was the rabbits and their pens that needed attention. I watched the moth and wondered if it could see what was taking Dad so long.

Dad had already spent two of our Sundays building rabbit pens. They were made out of barn-board and chicken-wire and were attached to the back of the shed about four feet above the ground. They had light-weight flip tops for watering and feeding, as well as removable bottoms for easy cleaning. Dad had made them simple so that Grandpa could manage them, but after a week of use Grandpa called to complain. His voice was deep, raspy and loud. He was drunk again.

"Where's your dad?" He shouted.

I picked up a notepad and pen. "He's gone to the store."

"Well get a pen and write this down!"

"Okay, go ahead."

"Ya got a pen?"

"I have a pen, Gramp."

"Okay, now get this all down. It's about them rabbit pens! The latches are too small for my hands. I got arthritis, ya know? And the pens are too low. My back's sore enough without havin' to bend all the time! And them bottoms are handy for cleanin', but so damned heavy that I end up dumpin' rabbit shit all over myself! I can't piss around with rabbits when they're set up like that. Specially not the way my heart's been actin' up!"

"That it?"

"Yeah, that's it! What the hell's your dad tryin' to do anyways, kill me?"

"I don't know, I'll ask."

"Ya gettin' smart with me?"

"No, Grandpa. I'll pass this along."

So it was another Sunday and Dad was behind the shed, tending to rabbits and pens. I was on the deck waiting to go fishing. It was hot and sticky and I was thirsty so I got up and went inside to the kitchen. It was a pale yellow room. The walls were all hinges and knobs, cupboards from top to bottom jam-packed with everything from candy bars and rubber bands to potatoes and Preparation H. The table was a heavy-duty oak job with thick square legs. Sometimes after a half dozen beers or so, Grandpa liked to remind me of its solidity, that he built it himself back in '63. It was nicked and marred, stained and cracked, but Grandpa insisted that all it needed was a "refinishin' job". All I could see was another Sunday slipping away with Dad sanding and painting.

I sat at one end of the table sipping murky lemonade, while Grandpa was at the other end cleaning under his fingernails with a jackknife. I wondered if he was digging out rabbit shit.

"What's Dad doing, building more pens?"

"Just drink your lemonade. I went to the trouble of makin' it for Chrissakes."

Grandpa's hair was iron gray, slicked back and shiny. His steel-blue eyes were disguised beneath wrinkled slits and Coke-bottle lenses. Grandpa looked like a man who had been 300 pounds one day and 150 the next. His cheeks sagged, his skin was loose and droopy. It shook and trembled when he moved. He wore red suspenders, a checkered flannel shirt, and dirty jeans. Grandpa's end of the table was marked with Lite beer cans, a jar of Planter's unsalted nuts, and a bottle of Bayer aspirin. All on account of his heart, he said.

The lemonade was cloudy and whitish-yellow. I pushed it away from me.

"I don't want anymore."

Grandpa set the knife down, picked up a beer and gulped some of it down. Then he started fumbling with the nut jar. It took him about a minute to get it open. The cap fell onto his lap. He shook some nuts into his palm, a few scattered onto the floor. He picked up the cap, got it screwed back on, then rolled the jar across the table to me. I shoved it back at him. A deep wrinkle creased its way between his bushy, black eyebrows. Grandpa was pretty loaded.

"You're a real tough one, aren'tcha?"

"No, I just don't want any nuts."

I pushed my chair back and started to get up. "I'm gonna go out and check on Dad."

Grandpa leaned forward and put his arms on the table. "Didn't your dad tell ya to mind me?"

I settled back into the chair. He leaned back again and tossed the handful of nuts at his mouth. Most of them went in, two or three fell down the front of him. He picked one out of his shirt pocket, another out of his crotch and ate them. He lifted one of the beer cans and shook it. A little beer left inside sloshed around. He raised the can to his lips, his hand was crooked, blotchy, shaking. He tilted his head back and slugged down the rest of the beer. His throat was purple, veiny, hanging flesh. I could smell him, all beer and nuts, and it made me fidget in my chair.

He burped then asked, "So, what they teachin' ya in school nowdays?"

"It's summer vacation."

"I meant when you do go, smartass!"

"Well, one of the last things we studied was reproduction."

"And they wonder what's wrong nowdays!"

"Reproduction in frogs, Gramp."

He leaned forward onto the table and made a steeple with his hands.

"Being a smartass, are ya?"

"No. It really was frogs!"

"You're a damned smartassed kid and ya think that the world evolves around ya!"

"Revolves," I said.

"What?"

"It's REVOLVES, not EVOLVES."

Grandpa slammed his palms onto the table. "Don't backtalk me, ya lil' shit!"

I got up to leave and yelled, "You're being crazy!"

Grandpa stood up. "What you need is a good asswhippin'! Get back in that chair!"

The corner of his mouth quivered, it was white with spittle. I backed toward the door. I was hot, my stomach was butterflies.

"No! I'm gonna go see what's taking Dad so long!"

He came forward, grabbed my shoulder with one hand and backhanded me with the other. His hand was heavy and strong against my temple. I'd never been hit before. I wrenched free and grabbed the doorknob. He steadied himself against the edge of the table.

"Git back here, ya lil' prick!"

"Fuck you!" I said.

He was red, then purple, then falling to the floor. I flung open the door and ran toward the woodshed, my nose and lungs all lilacs. The sun had moved down in the sky, the air was cooler, crickets were sawing away.

Dad had always said the fishing was better near nightfall. He said he and Grandpa used to catch the biggest bass just as the sun fell below the horizon, when it dimmed to an orange glow. By then, he said, the air was cool and the water calm. It was feeding time. Bats and swallows would dive and dart, skimming the water's mirrored surface, all in the name of bugs. Hungry bass would leap free. Up and out of the water they'd fly, bodies shimmering in fading daylight, breaking the smooth surface in hopes of nabbing an unsuspecting bug. Their eruptions and landings would create ringed ripples that took forever to disappear. Dad would be at the bow, Grandpa at the stern. Grandpa's boat, Dad said, was a potpourri of fish, peanuts and beer. The darkened shoreline would be alive with whippoorwills, owls, and the flickering eyes of campfires. I wanted nothing more than to go fishing with Dad.

The rabbit pens were all open and empty. Dad was wiping off the hatchet with a rag. Behind him, Bo was nosing over a pile of bloodied fur, guts and rabbit heads. Nailed along the back of the shed, above the pens, were naked hollow bodies dripping blood. I felt heavy and sick.
"Aw Christ, Jackie! I told Gramp to keep ya inside!"
"Dad…"
"Jackie listen, we'll talk about this when we go fishin' tonight, I swear."
All I could think of was what I had done.
"Dad…Gramp fell."
He dropped the rag and the hatchet. He ran away up the steps, onto the deck and disappeared into the house. Bo stuck his head into the pile, snatched up a hunk of something reddish purple and trotted away. Mosquitoes hummed secrets in my ears.

Fishing

Waves rocked the boat. The fish stringer rattled. I was watching the three bass we had caught float up and down. Their movements were in slow-motion and graceful. Their breathing was slow and synchronized; gills opening and closing, opening and closing. They were weaker and a darker green than they had been an hour or so before.

I felt wrong about everything.

Uncle Rick's voice was heavy and near, too near.

"How's them fish doin'?" he asked.

I couldn't look at him. My eyes were fixed on the biggest bass. I was thinking about how exciting it had been catching him the way he took the bait then erupted out of the water in a great splash. I was thinking of how much he had fought, how my heart had been electrified when he darted left, then right, then down deep below the boat. I was sure that the line was going to snap, that he'd spit the hook, that I would lose him, but I didn't. Uncle Rick was behind me the whole time, coaching, helping me bring the fish in. He told me to take my time, to work the fish, to tire him out, but I reeled as fast as I could.

When I thought about the way Uncle Rick was there, behind me, hands on my shoulders, helping, my insides moved. The bass looked smaller now as he floated sideways in the water.

"Maybe we ought to let them go," I said.

"But you really wrestled that big one."

I felt another fish tugging my line and jerked the bait away. I didn't feel like fishing anymore.

"So, you like that new rod I got ya?" he asked.

I reeled in then tossed the bait farther away. "It casts real good."

"It's supposta be unbreakable too."

The sunshine on the waves looked like strands of tinsel drifting. My eyes were tired from squinting. The glare was bright and hot. My shoulders and face burned. I heard Uncle Rick behind me thumping around near the outboard. He slid the gas tank out from under his seat to check the fuel level. I was hoping that it was almost empty, that there was just enough gas to get back to shore. Then I heard him monkeying with the cooler, shuffling it around.

"Hey, I almost forgot…" his movements were loud and clumsy, he nearly tipped us over, "…I made your favorite. Submarine sandwiches!"

My stomach growled.

"I'm not hungry."

"Whatever you say, but I made them if you want them."

The sun disappeared behind a cloud and my skin was relieved. I opened my eyes wide and stared out over the lake. Green waves began to roll. Three seagulls were bobbing up and down in the middle of the lake. A yellow waverunner skipped across the water behind them, but the birds didn't move. I watched the yellow machine disappear into the shoreline of boats, docks, rafts and cottages. Behind me, Uncle Rick cracked open another beer, number nine on the afternoon. I knew that it wouldn't be long before we'd be off cruising across the lake toward the bay.

Black Gully Bay was secluded, calm and peaceful. Its shoreline was thick with trees, rotten stumps and tall weeds. The air there was infested with mosquitoes and blackflies. The water was dark and deep. I'd seen all sorts of creatures there, snakes, turtles, minnows and frogs, but never once had I seen or caught a fish. The bay was always Uncle Rick's idea. He liked it because we were alone.

I felt another fish tugging my line and pulled the hook away. Thunder rumbled in the distance.

"Sounds like a storm," I said.

I set aside the rod and turned around. Uncle Rick was staring at me. I looked away from him to the sky. A trio of enormous, purple-gray clouds were rolling in over the lake. I almost felt happy.

"Why look at you!" He said as he reeled in his line. "You're really startin' to fill out."

I snatched my shirt off the seat and pulled it on. His eyes were wide, bloodshot and watery. Since he had been squinting against the sun's glare most of the day his red eyes were circled with white. It looked like he was wearing a mask. His fleshy, round cheeks were tomato red. He smiled and winked at me.

The wind was gusting now, the waves higher.

"We really should be heading in, don't ya think?"

He took a drink of beer as the boat humped over a big wave.

"We can't head in yet, we ain't been in the bay."

Beer dribbled down his chin onto his chest. A few curly black hairs stood out against the edge of his yellow tank top. His arms, shoulders and bald head were red. He tossed the empty can under his seat and it, along with the other empties, began to roll back and forth. Waves were breaking against the boat. The stringer was rattling. Three sinkers and a red-and-white bobber rolled out from under the seat and joined the action. Everything was moving. Thunder grumbled again, and this time it was closer.

"Uncle Rick, there's a storm comin'."

"Just sit down, we're headin' to the bay."

His voice was deep and scratchy, borderline angry. I sat down and looked out over the lake. The seagulls were high in the sky, white dots flying toward the place where the waverunner had disappeared. The sky was heavier, lower, darker. Thunder boomed again and I wondered why God wasn't sending any lightning. Not to hurt or kill, but to save.

A light blue pontoon boat chugged by, splashing through white-capped waves. An old man wearing a white hat and white T-shirt was at the steering wheel. He was so tan he looked black. He waved. Uncle Rick returned the gesture then started the motor.

I leaned over, pulled the stringer up and held the fish alongside the boat as we headed toward the bay. I let the water splash over them, hoping that they would hold on for a little while longer. Their gills moved, but their bodies dangled lifeless at the end of the chain. I felt sorry for them and angry at myself for fishing. Their eyes were black and in them I could see the sky; the shadowy clouds drifting by. The motor was loud and grating as the boat thudded across the lake breaking waves, and the water splashed me. The drops were cold like ice, but I didn't move. I was lost in the motor's mechanized drone, staring into the eyes of fish I felt dying.

Uncle Rick cut the engine. We coasted into the bay. I felt numb as the sound of the motor remained, buzzing all over inside me. I plopped the bass into the water. They jerked to life for a moment then fell still. I noticed their gills moving more rapidly.

"You haven't told anyone about our fishin', have you?"

"No."

The bay was calm and dark. The air was thick with insects. The shore was black with trees and weeds. The crickets were loud, their chirping unsettling. I wanted to jump overboard and swim away, swim out of the bay, swim across the lake toward the shore of boats, docks, cottages, and rafts. I looked over the side into the water and could see myself. I was flat and dark—a shadow.

"You know how much this means to me, don'tcha buddy?"

The clouds shook. A raindrop hit my head. I felt a needling pain in my ankle and knew it was a fly. I wondered why they always took to biting before a storm and if there were more why they couldn't carry me away and eat me. Two more raindrops hit me, one on the knee, the other on my back.

"I can't do this anymore," I said.

He moved to the middle seat.

"But I'm nice to you, ain't I? I got ya that rod. I made your favorite food. You're my fishin' buddy."

He put his hand on my leg. I wanted to pull away, but didn't want him to grab me. His fingers moved up my thigh. "It's just like this, then you do the same for me."

The sky broke and the rain fell hard against the lake, against the boat, against me. Thousands of drops were coming down drowning away everything.

"Don't touch me."

His hand gripped my thigh.

"What did you say?"

"Leave me alone."

My heart pounded and I trembled. He stood and pulled me off of my seat, toward him. I pushed him away and the boat rocked. I could hear the rain falling like BBs and I could hear the bobber, the sinkers, the cans, all rolling around beneath me.

He put his mouth against my ear.

"All I do for you and this is how you repay me?"

His breath was hot and smelled of beer. He held my shoulder with one hand and tried to unbutton my shorts with the other. I pushed him off balance and he fell over the middle seat onto the empty cans.

"You ungrateful little bastard!"

He got up and lunged toward me. I grabbed my fishing rod and hit him in the head. It broke in two, I let go, and the pieces fell over the side. He pushed me into my seat. The boat rocked more violently. His mouth was wide, his breathing heavy. Rain streamed down his red face. He looked like a candle melting. He leaned over me and tried to push me all the way down. I kicked him and his fall was slow motion. He went over in a backward somersault, arms flailing. The back of his head slammed against the edge of the boat. I held to my seat so I wouldn't go over.

I sat up as the boat settled. The rain poured down and the surface of the lake was all bubbles and foam. I couldn't see him anywhere. Thunder erupted all around and lightning crackled through the bruised sky. I waited, but he was gone. I sat down and breathed. I felt released and empty. Shaking, through raindrops and tears, I reached over the side and unhooked the fish. They plunged into the water and were gone.

Merry Christmas

Grandma hollers from the kitchen, "Somebody better go upstairs and check on Kelly, I think she's crying."

I'm 12 years old sitting on the big green velour couch feeling itchy. I'm wearing this new Christmas sweater Mom bought me to wear to Grandma's. It's red with little white snowmen on it. I can barely stand it. My brothers, Dustin and Dan, are sitting with me peering into the pile of gifts that are under the tree. We're waiting to dive into the goodies to see what we'll come away with this year. I see one of mine wrapped in newspaper and I don't even have to guess who it's from. Aunt Jane, the recycling queen, has stashed these beauties all over under the tree. Some are wrapped in editorials, some in the finance section, and some in the sports pages. Mine's half comics, half A&P ad. The Peanuts Gang is on the side facing me, Hillshire Christmas Hams are on the top. My name is printed neatly in thick red letters on a piece of white masking tape that runs over Snoopy's ear. The newspaper-wrapped boxes are all the same shape and size. Aunt Jane works at Lancaster's shoes and can't stand to see a Nike box go to waste.

Aunt Sarah and Uncle Bob are late as usual and all of us are stuck waiting on them. I hear Aunt Tammy chirping to Uncle Tom about Aunt Kelly and I'm wondering what's going on. Aunt Tammy's round, rouge-coated cheeks are jiggling like canned cranberry sauce as she talks to Uncle Sam. I can tell by her lowered voice that whatever she's saying about Aunt Kelly it must be scandalous. Uncle Sam is shaking his head and picking his nose. Aunt Tammy stops talking just long enough to slap his hand then keeps right on chirping.

"I'll go check on her," Aunt Jane says.

I'm still wondering what's up and look to my Dad. He's talking to Uncle Jake. Uncle Jake, of course, is drinking. I see he's getting loopy and I'm thinking about how hard it must be for Dad. They both have gold-rimmed glasses, reddish-blond hair and graying beards. Their resemblance is remarkable. The only difference this year is that Dad's hand is without the shiny, aluminum beer can.

Grandma comes wobbling into the family room. One hand holding her glass of wine, the other her cigarettes. She's wearing Levi's and a pink, fuzzy sweater that sort of just hangs over her bony frame. She's got one of the glowing sticks in her mouth. Through some puffs of smoke she comments on the tree.

"Kids, I think this is the best tree yet."

I look to my brothers and they're laughing. The tree looks like a bush wrapped in aluminum foil with all the gaudy tinsel. Our laughter is cut short though by our cousin Jesslyn. She's wearing an emerald dress with white stockings. She looks cute and all, but it's a look that's definitely deceiving. I try to look past her, searching for other boxes that belong to me, but she starts waving her hands in my face.

There's some thumping upstairs and the family room shakes. Everyone looks up at the silver chandelier hanging in the middle of the ceiling. Dangling from it, on about a foot of fishing line, is a golden angel holding a harp. It has a wiry halo over its head and bells dangling from its feet. The more thumping there is, the more the angel sways. Everyone is silent. I'm just waiting for the whole unit to come crashing down, or at the very least for the bells to ring. The silence between the thumping is terrible. I can hear Grandma's wheezy breathing and outside ice is cracking against the windows. Mixed in with a series of heavy thumps is a horrendous crash, like a dozen glass bowls being dropped, then suddenly all is quiet upstairs. In seconds everyone is going about Christmas business as usual.

"Is Aunt Kelly okay?" Jesslyn asks, waving her chubby arms in front of my face.

"I don't know," I say.

My brother Dan, leans forward and shoves her. "Get out of here, you little dork!"

Jesslyn falls back into the coffee table and knocks a dish of red and green M&M's onto the floor. She starts bawling like crazy so Mom gets up from the recliner and pops me in the back of the head. It doesn't hurt, but it messes my hair enough so that Dustin starts laughing at me. I'm more embarrassed than anything so I slug him. Mom pops me in the back of the head again.

"Jesus, Ma! I didn't do anything."

"You're the oldest, you should know better!"

"Better than what?"

"Don't get lippy with me, mister. I've got enough on my mind already than to be worrying about what you kids are doing."

I think about asking what's up with Aunt Kelly, but decide against it. Intoxicated Uncle Jake is peeved at his cute little daughter for knocking over the candy. Through a slur of syllables he orders her to pick them up. I smile to myself for this moral victory and look to Mom for an apology. She's eyeing up Dad though, thinking about last Christmas no doubt, wondering if maybe this is the year Dad's going to stay sober. Uncle Jake hands his can to Dad then returns to scolding Jesslyn. Dad stares at the beer can like he's never seen one before. His lips disappear beneath his thick mustache. I wonder if maybe he's licking them.

"You boys have to sit there and wait. When Aunt Sarah and Uncle Bob show up, we'll open presents. Until then, you'll sit and behave if you know what's good for you."

Mom says all of this without taking her eyes off Dad. Tension is about as thick as the smoke rolling from the cigarette on Grandma's lips. I'm still watching Dad. My gaze is fixed on that silver can. I start thinking back to last year when Dad was so drunk Mom and Uncle Jake had to take him to the hospital.

Everybody was talking in whispers that Christmas. Dad was stumbling around the presents, joking about Aunt Jane's "fancy wrappin' papers" when he fell. I remember him there, his body kind of jerking around and Mom shoving her fingers down his throat to get him breathing again. I wasn't scared until Grandma started crying, just numb. As soon as Grandma started though, my throat tightened. I held on a bit longer until Dustin, then Dan began to cry. Then the three of us slid as close together as we could on the green couch and bawled. Aunt Kelly came over to us and sat down. I crashed my head into her shoulder, closed my eyes and plugged my ears. The only thing I remember after that was Grandma waking me up with her cigarette breath and a plate of Chewy Chips Ahoy cookies.

"Jesslyn honey, it's okay, don't cry."

Grandma's voice snaps me out of the Christmas before and I'm glad. Her knees are cracking and popping as she lowers herself to help Jesslyn pick up M&M's. Before I know it, I'm down there too. Mom tells Grandma to sit down and relax, but Grandma ignores her. Instead, she stretches one of her bony arms into the darkness under the coffee table, cracks some more, and comes up with three reds and two greens. I'm thinking about asking Grandma about Aunt Kelly, but the late ones finally show up and Grandma groans her way back to her feet.

They come stomping into the house like cows, snow flying everywhere. I pick up one last M&M, see that Jesslyn is watching me and toss it into my mouth with a smile. She tries to tell on me, but Mom's already heading to greet the blizzard people. Grandma doesn't notice either. She's busy lighting another cancer stick and sizing up her wine.

"Merry Christmas!" Uncle Bob yells.

Uncle Jake mumbles to Dad, "It's about goddamned time."

Aunt Sarah makes up an excuse for being late and it's better than last year's anyway. They make the rounds, hugging, kissing, shaking hands—all that cordial jazz and I'm looking out the window. I can hear the snow, ice more like it, cracking against the thick panes of glass. It sounds like someone's throwing pebbles. I can't see though, it's too dark.

So here we are; the whole family. My brothers and I are waiting for the goods, but Aunt Kelly is still upstairs. Suddenly, the talking stops, cigarette smoke seems to freeze in mid-air, and all eyes are on Aunt Jane as she stands in the doorway. Dustin's a smart-ass and notices the mistletoe over her head.

"Fat chance for her gettin' a kiss," he says.

I laugh and Mom scowls at me. Aunt Jane opens her mouth.

"Okay, everyone. Kelly's coming down. Act normal!"

I'm lost. I don't know why I'm supposed to act normal and I glance over at Dad for some direction. He sees me, smiles, and tips his hand in a drinking motion. Only his hand is empty. I'm confused and keep watching. He goes round and round with his pointer finger by his ear doing the "crazy" motion. Suddenly, Aunt Kelly comes down. Down like a sack of potatoes. She's tumbling down the stairs. I can hear her and I can't believe my ears. She falls down to our level and nobody goes to help her. Dustin and Dan are giggling and I'm trying not to bust.

Aunt Kelly gets up like nothing has even happened. Her eyes are red, her sweater's inside-out. She tries to walk, but wobbles like Grandma and I know what's wrong. She's drunk.

She manages a "Maherry Carissmis!", staggers into the room then plops herself onto the floor in front of the tree. My cousin, Jesslyn, is pestering my brothers as Aunt Kelly fumbles around trying to pass out gifts. I'm looking around for Mom, for some answers, but she's missing. Invisible pebbles are still being tossed at the window behind me. I look outside, but still can't see a thing. I hear Aunt Jane and Aunt Tammy whispering, "Everyone should just leave Kelly alone."

Uncle Jake is offering Dad a beer, Grandma's praising the tinsel tree, and Mom comes in with a coffee mug in her hand. She walks over to Dad, hands him the steaming mug and kisses his cheek.

"I'm Sahntah Closs thish yahear!" Aunt Kelly shouts.

Mascara is smudged all over under her eyes like she's been crying. Ruby red lipstick is smeared on her cheek like crayon and her fly is wide open showing off her satiny white underwear.

Dad is staring at Aunt Kelly. Mom is staring at Dad. He lifts the mug to his lips and I can't help but notice the trembling of his hand.

An Accident

It was hard not glancing at her breasts every other telephone pole or so knowing that they were right there with me on the front seat of my 1981 Ford Fairmont. My car, my royal blue, luggage-racked, six cylinder beast; my beast and my breasts. Sixteen years old with my very own station wagon. Who could believe it? Those breasts were mine to have and to hold whenever the gas gauge needle was anywhere above empty.

The sun was a flaming eye beaming through the bug-gutted windshield. The Fairmont was an oven. I was wondering how long it would be before Stacey and I melted away, before we became just another stain on the bench seat. Coffee, soda, ketchup, cheese, Stacey and me. Sweat dribbled out from under my arms, from above my ears and behind my knees. I tried to look at Stacey's face, but she was gazing into the mirror, checking for makeup smudges no doubt.

🍁 🍁 🍁

We always had some destination. The record shop. The mall. Dairy Queen for peanut buster parfaits in the summer. Big Boy for cocoa in the winter. No matter where we started we ended up someplace else. Sometimes it was behind the hockey rink. Sometimes it was down an abandoned dirt road. Most of the time though it was at the boat harbor during lunch break. Out of class and off to the 7-11 for Big Gulps and nachos then to the harbor. We'd park between rows of yachts August through October, behind the public toilets November through April then back between the yachts till July. We'd eat together, but I always finished first. I wanted time to chew some gum, or gargle some soda before we started messing around. I was the real romantic type. Stacey though, who prided herself on big hair and layers of makeup, didn't worry much about oral hygiene. She had braces, wiry-steel teeth, that collected everything. Her mouth was half digested food particles. Her tongue was cold and slimy. I'd close my eyes, hold my breath and think of the neighbor girl, Mandy, as I squeezed and kneaded Stacey's breasts.

Mandy was two years older than me and up until she graduated we had shared a seat on the bus every morning. Her hair was long and brown, fresh and wild, like spring. Her cheeks were naturally pink, her eyes warm, dark-brown and inviting. I remembered the morning Mandy got on the bus and handed me her purse. It was a big, saddlebag kind of deal with horses etched into the leather. She took off her coat, settled into the seat and told me she was dead tired. She had been up all night with cramps. The bus started rolling and I was still holding her purse when her body began to sway. The bus bounced and shimmied, but she was falling asleep anyway. Her body inched closer and closer to mine. I watched her breathe. Her arm fell on my knee. Without warning, her body jerked twice and came to life. She opened her eyes and asked if she'd been sleeping.

On this particularly hot June day, I talked Stacey into skipping lunch, ditching afternoon classes and heading out to my house. The sun was glaring into the Fairmont, baking. I needed air. I was fumbling with the window to get just the right amount of airflow so that I could breathe, but not so much as to mess Stacey's hair. She hated the wind messing her hair. At times, her beauty could be a real pain. If she wasn't checking her look in a mirror, she was doing double takes in shop windows. I hated the way she'd watch her reflection wiggle up to the 7-11 in those huge glass windows. I swear, if she could have watched herself walk from the wagon to the nacho counter all day, she would have.

Another thing that got me sore was that she was always messing with the Fairmont's mirrors. If she wasn't fidgeting around gawking at her face in the passenger side mirror, she was screwing with the rearview mirror. It was pretty sickening the way she loved herself so much. Anyway, while I fumbled with the window she reached over and started screwing with the air conditioner. Another thing I hated—her reaching. She was always reaching over to scan radio stations, to angle the vents, to put in or take out cassette tapes. She'd reach to turn up the heat, to turn down the heat, to click, turn, twist and fumble with whatever she could. It was all I could do not to slap her hand some days. But, the way she leaned, her body at the end of her seatbelt, the belt giving those breasts an even larger, rounder appearance, the smell of Electric Youth and hairspray—the scent that became my own on most days because we couldn't separate—mesmerized me.

In a millisecond, the Fairmont was onto the shoulder of the road pushing around gravel. The rear of the car went nuts and we just about smacked a cow-shaped mailbox. I gave the wheel a few cranks, first left, then right, then left again. Stacey's head banged the passenger side window each time. I straightened us out and kept going. She looked in the mirror, patted her hair, but didn't say a word. Instead, she went right on reaching, scanning, twisting, clicking and turning. It wasn't until she got the air conditioner going full blast and the Fairmont could barely breathe that she seemed happy. She nuzzled my ear as we cruised by a curve-ahead sign. It was a yellow blur. She eased her hand onto my leg. We went into the curve, the Fairmont chugging at 65. Stacey stroked my thigh. The bald tires skidded through the corner. I had her breasts in the corner of my eye as we roared out of the curve. I was praying to God that nobody would be home, that my folks were still working, that my sister had run off with her boyfriend. I eased on the brakes as we came to my road. I was praying that Stacey and I could be alone. I was praying so hard that I almost missed the sight of Mandy's pickup truck bouncing through the field. Not just bouncing, but flipping end over end, throwing chunks of sod, pieces of metal, flying.

The truck was in mid-flip when I saw Mandy soaring through the air. The truck fell forward after her. When it came to rest, I was already out of the Fairmont through the ditch and high-stepping through Queen Anne's lace. I almost broke my neck on the spare tire. It took my feet out from under me and I landed on her purse. It was the same purse I had held dozens of times, sometimes so she could take off her coat, sometimes so she could put it on. It was awkward and heavy, but I would have carried it through the school lunchroom at noon had she asked me.

I stood up, purse in hand and listened. One of the truck's tires buzzed as it wobbled round and round, tread rubbing against part of the fender. The sun was hot. The radiator hissed. A cow mooed. I listened closer, wanting to call out her name, but afraid I wouldn't get an answer. The truck's radio was still playing. "I got you babe, I got you babe..." My armpits dripped. The air was gasoline mixed with cow manure. I knew I had seen her being thrown from the truck. I knew that I had seen her long brown hair spread out all around her as she floated forever about eight feet in the air. I knew it, but checked inside the truck anyway.

Blood outlined the edges of a hole in the driver's side window. Droplets peppered the seat, the ceiling, the instrument panel. I felt a little relieved though because I had thought there'd be more. Sonny and Cher belted out one last "I got yooooo, babe!" and the DJ started in about a thunderstorm warning. The sun was high though, blazing. I backed away from the truck and listened. I was sure I wouldn't hear her.

Then, it came. A rustle-thumping sound, a body in the tall grass, thrashing. I ran toward it. The purse banged against my leg. Mandy was trying to get up, to right herself, but her legs wouldn't let her. Both of them were twisted and mashed. It was hard to tell where jeans ended and flesh began. She looked at me, but without recognition. Her eyes were glazed, the left one half closed, already swelled up from a blue ball that was pressing out from the inside of her head. The DJ was still talking. *Due to strong winds and golf ball sized hail, people in Arenac county should take cover immediately.* Cows were moving along the far edge of the field, grazing and watching. An airplane buzzed overhead. Grasshoppers took to flight as Mandy pushed herself up with her left arm. The arm was white and clean, untouched. It was the same arm that had handed me the purse, the same one that had touched my knee, the same arm that made me blush. She wobbled silently, then fell. Pieces of grass, Queen Anne's lace, and dirt fell from her hair. I watched her breathing. She closed her eyes and her body jerked twice. It was the same involuntary muscle movement I had witnessed one morning as we sat, half-dozing, our bodies warm and touching as the school bus rattled down rutty dirt roads. This time though, she was still.

Flies circled and buzzed her. One landed on her cheek. A red and white Igloo cooler rested beside her. It too had been tossed from the truck. It was sitting upright, ready, as if expecting a picnic to be had in the vast, open field. I didn't hear Stacey behind me, but felt her approaching. I could smell hairspray and Electric Youth. Thunder boomed. The sun was swallowed by a cloud. Stacey tugged at the purse in my hand and it just about killed me.

The Horn

The snow had been coming all day, first in flurries, then in steady heavy wet flakes. It was good packing snow, so I was making snowballs and throwing them at the cows. Not throwing to hit them, but to see how they'd react. The only one that paid any attention was Cybil, the old white cow. She stared at me as the snowballs landed all around her. Her eyes dark and unblinking. She wouldn't move and it looked liked someone had walked out into the field and made a cow out of snow.

The other cows had their heads buried in hay. Each of them were wearing white blankets of snow on their backs. At five, when Tom's Chevette came sliding into the driveway, Cybil put her head down and walked over to the others.

I got in the car and stomped off my feet.

"Why ya gotta bring all that shit in here?" Tom asked.

"The snow? Well, if you haven't noticed, it's a goddamned blizzard out there."

"So, you coulda stomped off outside."

"In the snow? What good would that do?"

Tom's face was windburn. He was wearing a red and black checkered, wool hunting hat. It had long hanging earflaps and a drooping brim. He had the strings of the earflaps tied up under his orange beard.

"You owe two bucks."

"For what?" I asked.

"Beer."

"What beer?"

Tom reached over the seat and came away with two bottles of Pabst. We popped off the tops with our seatbelts and clanked the bottles together.

"A cheer," Tom said.

I looked out the window at Cybil the cow. She was chewing and watching us go.

"To Cybil," I said.

"I'm not drinking to a cow."

"Why not?"

"Cause she'll probably be steak before too long."

"Cybil's not an eater, she's a milker."

Tom shook his head, spun us around in a donut then headed us out of the driveway. The snow was piling up like mad, coming down so heavily that Tom had us slowed to a crawl.

"Fucking snow," he said.

"Where'd you get the beer?"

"From Stan."

"Stan Kowalski?"

"Yep, Stan the man."

"Stan, what a dope. How'd you convince him to buy for us?"

"I gave him Emily Thompson's number."

"You even got her number?"

"What do you think?"

"I think you don't."

Tom turned on the headlights and cranked up the heat. The Chevette's engine sputtered.

"Kowalski's a dick. He'll think he wrote down the wrong number or something." Tom chugged down the beer.

"So what are you gonna tell him when finds out it's not hers? When he gets his big Pollock paws on you and is ready to beat your ass?"

"I told him I got the number from you."

"You asshole! What am I gonna do?"

"I don't know. You're a goddamned Pollock, he ain't gonna hurt you. You dumb bastards all stick together."

"Oh blow it out your ass! What are you? A goddamned German? I'm surprised this fuckin' heater ain't cranked up to 350 degrees, like an oven."

"What's that supposed to mean?"

"Nevermind."

"You talkin' about the Jews?"

"Nevermind."

"Man, that's bogus. An oven. You're one sick bastard, Kausabowski."

I put the Pabst to my lips and sucked it dry.

"Where do you want the empties?" I asked.

"Save em' for the horn," Tom said as he turned us left onto Oldfield Street. We fishtailed around the corner. I opened another beer.

Tom and I had always traveled the horn. Weekend, weeknight. Summer, spring, winter, fall. We'd hop in his Chevette and drive the horn, a rough stretch of road that ran off behind the Clifton Cement Plant and alongside Misery Bay. The going was slow no matter what, but since it was winter and snowing like hell, the going was even slower.

The road was really named Northpoint Road, but we called it The Horn because about halfway into our trip there was this driveway with a big red ship horn at the end of it. When we neared it, I'd take whatever empties were handy, lean out the window and see if I could throw them into the opening. It wasn't easy because Tom would either speed up or slow down and swerve all over so I couldn't get my timing right. More often than not, the bottle ended up shattering against the horn and the pieces fell into the driveway. It didn't matter, Tom said, because the place at the other end of the driveway was just a summer cottage anyway. Owned by some software engineer from Farmington Hills.

Tom and I drank a lot for a couple of kids. It wasn't a big deal for each of us to drink ten or twelve beers while cruising the horn. I never drove, Tom always did. The fact that his dad was an ex-lawyer turned mayor and that my dad worked at the cement plant had a bit to do with that. Tom's dad would bail him out if he got busted for drunk driving, whereas mine would have beat my ass. Dad didn't care so much that I drank, but he swore to God he'd kill me if I ever got caught drunk driving and I never argued the point because Dad had his reason.

It was two days before Christmas when Mom was on her way home from Fisher Big Wheel with a carload of gifts and Willie Lunker hit her head on. From what the papers had said Willie had worked the midnight shift and five hours of overtime then stopped at Kramer's Pub for a half dozen beers or so. He killed my mom with his Dodge in the early afternoon as she waited at a stoplight. I've seen the newspaper clipping. Our blue Plymouth station wagon crumpled up into a wad of metal. Fisher Big Wheel bags, new toys and clothing spread over the pavement. The only thing that makes Mom's death real besides the color of the car is the caption—*Scene of the crash, which claimed the life of 27 year old Alpena woman, Tabitha Kausabowski.*

I grabbed two more beers out of the backseat.

"Let's see if we can finish a few more of these before we get to the horn," Tom said.

I opened the beers and handed him one.

"What's the hurry?" I asked.

"This fuckin' weather's a bitch. If we get stranded out here it'd be nice to have a good buzz on."

The shoreline of Lake Huron was white. The sky was white. The Chevette trudged along pushing snow like a miniature plow. I could hear the car's bottom scraping along the road and feel the snow pounding against the floorboards. Tom steered with his knees. I reached down to turn on the radio.

"Don't turn that on."

"Why not?"

"Because, the less we got going, the less likely this thing will stall. I got the heat on and that's plenty. In fact…"

Tom reached down and turned down the heat.

"Now can we turn on the radio?" I asked.

"No, we got the headlights on and I didn't turn the heat off, I just turned it down."

"That's crazy. The radio's not gonna stall the car."

"Bullshit! I've been driving this car for two years! I know what I can and can't do!"

I sipped at my beer.

The road, its shoulders and the ditches were gone. Everything was lost beneath the snow. The windshield was beginning to fog so Tom switched the blower from heat to defrost.

"Aren't you afraid that sudden change in power is gonna stall us?"

"Go to hell, smartass."

"You're the one that's gonna go to hell, Tom. Lying to Stan. And then when Emily finds out that you gave out her number, she'll hate you too."

"Emily…what a dame, hey?"

"She's all right."

"What happened when you two went out?"

"Nothing."

"Don't give me that shit. What happened?"

I drank some more of my beer and held it up to Tom in the gesture of a toast so that he would shut up and drink.

"Fine. You don't want to talk. I pick you up everyday. I get us beer. I drive us around. I take all your verbal abuse and still you can't tell me what happened with Emily Thompson?"

"A gentleman never tells."

"Tells what? You said nothing happened."

I tried to look out over Misery Bay, but I couldn't see. I wondered if anyone had put their shanties out yet, and if they had, I wondered if the ice would be thick enough to hold a man, his shanty, and all of the snow.

"Your old man put his shanty out yet?" I asked.

"I know you're trying to change the subject. And I know you know that I love fishing and you're hoping to get me talking about fishing instead of what did or didn't happen between you and Emily."

Tom reached over the seat, still steering with his knees, and grabbed two more beers. The Chevette kept moving forward, pushing snow.

The horn was hardly ever plowed. The people who lived on Misery Bay and other parts of Lake Huron owned summer and winter cars. Acuras and Cadillacs for the steady, warm months. Land Rovers, Suburbans, and Cherokees for the cold, unpredictable months. Some of these folks even owned an extra truck, an old Dodge Ram or a Chevy Silverado. They were full-size and four-wheel-drive with tires bigger than they needed to be, and usually, they were outfitted with a winch and a plow. These trucks were used for "knocking around", as I'd heard them say. For towing fishing boats and motorbikes, for going to camp, and for keeping the pavement of their wide, winding driveways clear.

I thought of my Dad driving home in his old Ford F-150, the only vehicle he'd owned since the Plymouth he and Mom shared, and I knew that with all the snow it wouldn't be long before he'd be out there. He'd come home from work to eat then head out into the night to plow. Dad had his regulars that called. Old people who lived on the outskirts of town that didn't want to slip and fall while walking to the mailbox. Or sometimes, single and divorced women with lots of children. Women that were afraid of being snowed in because they could never tell when one of their kids was going to get sick or hurt. Dad told me that they'd invite him in for coffee or cocoa and on occasion, even dinner. Most of all, Dad figured people called for plowing because they were lonely.

Yes, Dad would be home now eating the stew I'd made. Venison stew with carrots, potatoes, and mushrooms. I'd left it on the woodstove, covered, so that it would be warm when he got home. I had made mashed potatoes too because I knew Dad liked to pour the stew over them. But I was disappointed because as me and Tom trudged along I remembered that on the note I'd left him that said, *'Went riding the horn with Tom. Checking for shanties'*, I'd forgotten to tell him that the mashed potatoes were on the second shelf behind the milk, in a foil-wrapped green dish. I wished then that one night he'd be lonely too, and that when I got home there'd be a message telling me that he'd be staying the night with one of those women because his truck had broken down.

Tom stopped the car. He shut off the wipers, the defrosters, left the Chevette idling, and started to get out.

"What are you doing?" I asked.

"I gotta piss."

"You just gonna leave the car here in the middle of the road?"

"Christ, ain't nobody coming. Nobody'll be down this road for another half hour. Not in this weather, anyway."

Tom slammed the door and jogged off the road into a stand of pines. I watched him until he vanished into the sagging, snow covered boughs.

I reached down and turned on the radio. There was nothing but static so I shut if off again and thought of the Saturday that Emily and I shared. The date I'd had that I couldn't share with Tom.

It had been a Saturday. It was cold, but nice and clear, and Emily had said she wanted to have a picnic. But it was the end of December and snow was on the ground, so I didn't believe it until I pulled into her driveway and she walked out of her house with a cooler and a backpack. It was hard pretending I wasn't surprised.

"What's in the cooler?"

I tried to take it from her and offered to take the pack, but she refused.

"It's a surprise, mister! You just keep your hands off!"

I went around and opened the trunk. I shoved aside my hunting rifle, my ice fishing rigs, and made room for the cooler by the spare tire.

"You hunt?" she asked.

"Yeah, but not much. I just like being outside, I guess."

"Sure, that's what they all say. Killing poor, helpless animals. You're all brutes, as far as I'm concerned." She smiled and got in the passenger side as I closed the trunk.

Emily looked classy. Her form fitting, gray wool coat. Her black hair hanging down and tucked around her neck like a scarf. She looked like a catalogue girl or some fresh faced t.v. actress crossing a busy city street, stopping traffic with her Herbal Essence hair. Me, well I'd been fishing the Pike run that morning and hadn't had time to shave or shower. I was wearing Sorrels, a quilted flannel, and a knitted hat. And as we rode out into the sunny fresh, snow covered country, and she talked about moving to Chicago to go to medical school, I wondered how it was that I had managed to land a date with her.

We had been in the car driving and talking for about an hour before we stopped.

"This is good," she said. "I like this place. It's pretty. What do you call it?"

"We call it Trumbull's Mill."

"Why's it called that?"

"It's the name of the guy that used to own the property. I'm not sure why they call it Mill though. I think it used to be a wood mill. You know, logging and stuff. In fact, if I'm not mistaken, this path we're on is an old logging trail. See how it dips down there to the stream?"

Emily unbuckled her seatbelt and leaned forward. She stared down to the place where the stream bubbled through the ice. My heater didn't work and she looked cold, so I was surprised when she untucked her hair from around her neck and began to unbutton her coat. She shrugged the coat off then tossed it into the backseat. Something fell from a pocket and onto the floor.

"What's that?" I asked.

"It's my cell phone. Never know when I'm going to need it, especially when parked in the woods with strange boys."

She giggled and smiled as she leaned down to pick up the phone. She put her hand on my leg and pulled herself back up into the seat.

"Use it much?"

"Not really. Only in emergencies."

She glanced back at the stream.

"It's an awfully small stream for logging."

"It used to be bigger. Wider. Since the cement plant put up their hunting club back in the woods, the water's slowed to a trickle here. Rumor has it that they've redirected the stream so that it flows through their property."

"Oh, it's not a rumor. It's true. I've seen it. I've stood in it. Up to my knees trying to catch crayfish. My Dad and his buddies are always out there drinking beer and playing cards. Sometimes I go back there to play with them. I'm surprised you've never been back there. Your dad does work at the plant, doesn't he?"

I pictured her dad and the rest of the Cement Plant execs. Wearing their khakis and their weekend hikers, drinking imported beer and talking about how they would head out at the crack of nine and make a killing, trolling Lake Huron with downriggers, depthfinders, and navigational systems on their boats named *Money Talks* or *Dollar's Wake*. And right then I knew that I wanted nothing to do with Emily Thompson. Not a picnic, not a conversation, not anything. And that's how I worked up the nerve to lean into her and give her pink fleshy lips a try.

Tom jumped into the car and it rocked from the weight of his body. Snow fell off him onto the steering wheel, onto the dashboard, and onto me. He was all lit up about something.

"You're not going to believe what I just fuckin' saw!"

"What?"

"A big, fat hound!"

"Who gives a shit?"

"Man, it was a hunting hound wearing a bright, red collar! And it had a bell around its neck or something because I could hear it jingling!"

"Bullshit! You're either getting drunk or going snow crazy."

"Goddammit! We should go find him!"

"What for?"

"We could probably stick one of these rich fucks for a reward, that's why! We could probably get fifty bucks for fat boy like him!"

"Tom, you're losing it. It's a hound. It's probably halfway home by now. You probably scared the shit out of it, stomping into the woods to take a piss."

"Come on, let's go!"

"No way! I thought we were gonna just drive the horn and drink and that's what I came to do. Besides, it's cold out and the wind's really starting to blow shit around. It's starting to drift and if we go traipsing through the woods we might end up lost. And I'm not freezing my ass off for some dog."

Tom shook his head.

"That's just it. You always got your head up your ass. Anytime some great opportunity comes along like this, you shirk it off. Like Emily. I bet you didn't even kiss her, did you?"

Both of us were quiet for a minute. We drank and listened to the wind as it blew up off the lake and screamed around the car. I could feel the Chevette rocking in the gusts.

"It's not letting up any. Maybe we should head back," I suggested.

"No, we're almost to the horn. Besides I gotta get the Emily scoop outta you yet."

"There's nothing to tell."

Tom leaned back in his seat and steered with his knees. "You should've seen that hound. A good hunting hound like that…I know we could get a reward. He had his damned face buried right in the snow. His nose stuck to the ground, pushing through snowdrifts! The bell ringing through all that snow. It was the prettiest thing I ever saw."

We drank more and moved along Misery Bay. I tried to look out my window and see shanties, but the glass was steamed up. Again I got to thinking of Emily.

Emily really had me going. My heart pounded against the seatbelt. The strap felt like it was burning through my clothes and into my chest. The air was stinking of sweat and dirty floorboards. The car was warm with our heat. The radio had been kicked on by a stray foot or leg and was buzzing a staticky song. Emily's body was pressed hard against mine. Her mouth was hot. Everything—the windows, the steering wheel, our bodies—was steamy and wet. Her hand was fighting my zipper and I wondered if she realized that I still had my seatbelt on.

One of her wild legs pounded the radio again and the staticky song buzzed louder. The heat, the stinking floorboards, Emily's hands pulling flesh and hair—all of it was suffocating. Finally, I unbuckled my seatbelt and eased the seat back to get enough distance from her so that I could take off my coat. By the time I had one arm out of its sleeve, Emily had unbuttoned her shirt and was shoving her naked breasts into my face. Their smell, something like a cross between oranges and baby powder was suffocating. I lifted her away from me to catch my breath and she stopped.

"What's wrong?" she asked.

"I couldn't breathe."

She leaned back against the steering wheel and covered herself with her arms.

I sat upright and tried to hug her. She shoved me back against the seat.

"You think I'm a whore, don't you?"

"What? No, I couldn't breathe is all."

"All you fucking guys think I'm a whore! That's why you ask me out! That's why you all drive me out to some fucking trail in the woods!"

She reached for her shirt and hit her head hard on the rearview mirror. Tears flooded her eyes. She scrambled to her seat, snatched up her phone and began to dial.

"What are you doing?"

"If you don't get us out of here and take me home this instant, I'm calling my father!"

Without another word between us I started the car, backed us out of Trumbull's Mill, and raced us back toward her house.

I can't remember if we said anything during the drive back, but I remember wanting to ask if she had any beer in the cooler, partly as an ice breaker, but partly because I was serious and thought both of us could use a drink. In the end, we got to her place and she was out of the car and heading into her house before I was even able to remind her to take her backpack and cooler.

I thought about keeping her stuff, but I knew better. Eventually, I would have to see her again and the date had been bad enough already. So I grabbed her pack and her cooler, and set them inside her old man's Land Rover. I made sure to open the bag first so that he could see her stash of condoms, then I left the cooler open too so that he would know who had been stealing the Dewar's from his liquor cabinet. With all that done, I looked at the sky and was thankful that it was still clear and light because that meant there was still plenty of time to go fishing.

Tom tossed his empty bottle into my lap and it startled me.

"We're almost there dipshit. Get ready."

I stuck a bottle on each finger of my left hand and held another one in my right. I turned sideways in the seat and opened the window. When I leaned out into the snow the wind felt like it was cutting my face and I could hardly breathe as snow rushed in all around me.

"Can't you block some of that shit from getting in?" Tom yelled.

"Just keep her steady!"

My eyes were watering like crazy and I blinked again and again to keep them from freezing. I could hardly see the big red horn through the swirling snow.

"How many bottles you got?" Tom asked.

"One in the barrel and five in the chamber!"

I dangled out the window and readied my aim. I could feel the cold in the bones of my hands and my skin felt like it was being pelted with rock salt. I could hear Tom yelling something, but it was drowned by the sound of wind howling.

We were about 25 yards from the horn when I let the first bottle go. It veered off to the right and was sucked away into the white. I reloaded quickly and threw two more. Both of them sailed over the horn and disappeared. Tom was yelling something to me again, it sounded like he was calling me "Hound Dog!" and suddenly the car was swerving all over the road. I dropped two of the bottles down the side of the car and as I struggled to get the last one off my thumb, Tom slammed on the brakes. My head crashed into the door frame as the Chevette jumped over something hard and spun sideways. Tom was yelling, "Hound! Hound!" and wrestling with the steering wheel as bottles, tools, and Tom's fishing gear went airborne all around me. My body lunged forward into the windshield and when I heard glass shattering I closed my eyes.

Tom started screaming and pounding his fists on the steering wheel. "Oh my God! It can't be!"

I was still, slumped against the dashboard, thinking of Mom, Dad, and Emily. What if it all had been different? If Mom hadn't died? If I hadn't forgotten to tell Dad about the mashed potatoes? If I had just gone and done it with Emily? I opened my eyes and could see blood on my hand. This was what it was like, I thought, to be dying. Then, I felt Tom punch me in the arm.

"Hey dumbass, get up! It's just a scratch!"

I sat up and looked around. Red and white fishing jigs stuck in the seat and carpet. The air was stinking like beer. Tom was out of the car, running down the road, back to the horn. I looked at my hand. Part of the bottle neck was still stuck on my thumb and blood was leaking from a small cut on my index finger. I felt the side of my head with my fingers and I could tell that by the time it was all said and done I'd have a good sized knot to contend with.

I got out of the car and started walking toward Tom. I could see the outline of his body like a shadow in the snow. He was knelt down in the middle of the road like he was praying. Ahead of him a ways I could see headlights shining fuzzy, like flashlights through a cotton sheet.

"What are you doing? There's a car coming! Get outta the road!"

Tom remained hunched over in the road. I looked back at the Chevette. It was sitting lopsided, up to the middle of its wheels in snow. I shoved my hands into my armpits for warmth and dragged my feet through the heavy drifts. Inside I felt something had happened and that something had been happening since I'd been standing at home, throwing snowballs at Cybil, waiting for Tom to show.

By the time I got to Tom I was numb, so seeing him there crying and touching the dead hound was strange. The dog's body was stretched out in the snow. Its eyes were closed and one long ear was flipped back over its head filling up with snow. Tom was fingering the shiny golden bell on the hound's collar.

"She won't be running no more," he said.

I knelt down beside him and the wind blew up all around us. Snow fluttered down the back of my neck and the chill of it felt good.

"I don't think that car is gonna see us, Tom. We better get her out of the road."

As Tom brushed the snow away from the hound's ear, I slid my arms under her and lifted her from the road. Besides a single spot of blood on the snow, all that remained was the imprint of her body. I watched Tom kick snow into it, then we walked off the road together. The dog was heavy and warm in my arms.

Tom came over to me and we watched the headlights come near. Three white faces peered through the windshield of a high-riding, black four-wheel-drive Dodge. It was a woman of about thirty with two small children. A boy and a girl. When I saw the woman's head drop and the children's mouths gape open at the sight of us, I knew that they must have been out looking in the storm for a long time. My eyes squinted and watered as the wind blew up into my face. My nose and lungs filled with snow and cold and I could hardly breathe as I wondered how I'd got there. I could've waited at home for Dad, then hopped in the plow truck with him. We could've been plowing driveways. Ones that belonged to old folks and lonely women. I could have went through it all with Emily and maybe I could've been at her house watching a movie on her big screen T.V., drinking the Dewar's she'd stolen from her old man. Or if there weren't such things as Christmas, Willy Lunker, or Fisher Big Wheel, I might be home with Mom. I tried to imagine her carrying a steaming kettle of mashed potatoes to the kitchen table, but it didn't work because I couldn't remember her.

Yellow

Grandma is yellow. Originally diagnosed as jaundice, her subsequent dizzy spells, fatigue and disorientation led to further testing which yielded this—Grandma is dying of liver cancer. She is yellow and has a few weeks to live.

I live six hundred miles away so I called her.

"Grandma, this is me, K.J."

In her polish accent, "I *know* who it is."

I can hear polka music and Grandpa pounding his cane on the floor. He's shouting, "Who is it, Lucy? Who is it?"

"Goddammit, Sylvester! Shut your mouth! I'm talking to our Grandson!"

"Which one?" Grandpa chimes.

"The only one that calls, you old fool! K.J.!"

"Did I call at a bad time?" I ask.

"No! No! This old fart's driving me crazy! Every time the phone rings he thinks it's a doctor with a miracle cure or that there was some mistake at the clinic. Can't he see? I'm yellow! I'm tired! I just want to sleep and he's in that kitchen bitching and banging his cane on the floor. Tap! Tap! Tap! Boom! Boom! Boom! The way he carries on I can't even watch golf on t.v.! I swear to God I'm going to shove that cane up his ass before it's all over!"

I can see her holding the phone against her big beautiful face. Her gray hair. Her small thin lips pursed and her little green eyes glaring through big oval glasses at Grandpa. I cannot for the life of me picture her as yellow.

I ask her, "How are you doing?" then think of how dumb I am. She's dying. That's how she's doing.

"I'm not dead yet!"

"That's good, hey?"

"I guess so…" She covers the phone, but I can still her yelling at Grandpa. "Turn down that radio and stop banging that cane or I'm going to beat you with it!"

Grandpa hasn't been handling it well. I learned this from my Mom. In fact, everything I know about Grandma's sickness has come from Mom. She's having a tough time too, but she's dealing with it. What's keeping Mom sane while watching her mother die is making the funeral arrangements. She says it's like planning a vacation for a person that will never return.

Grandma comes back to me. The music is quieter. Grandpa's not banging his cane.

"Sheesh! Finally, some peace!" she says, "Thank God!"

"What did you do to him, Grandma?"

"Your Uncle Dale came and got him. They're going to Posen to get some petunias. All I want is to sit on the porch in the summer sun and look at the flowers and birds."

I wonder if she's slipping away into thoughts of disarray. Summer is more than a few weeks away.

"That'll be nice. You always have the best flowers."

"So, what do you want?" Grandma asks, getting right to the point.

Her directness flusters me as always and I'm glad she can't see my face. I think my color would be insulting.

"I called because I was thinking of coming to visit."

"What? Don't be crazy! That's too long to drive!"

"But I want to see you before…" I cannot finish the sentence. The only sound is polka music and her breathing.

She's in her chair, I bet. In her burgundy recliner that never reclines. The t.v. is on, its shaky picture detailing the latest golf tournament. Always, she roots for Tiger Woods. "He's so damned cute!" she's said time and time again. In between sips of Milwaukee's Best, "Look at him. He sure can hit that ball. And the way he moves—so graceful!" The family thought maybe something was wrong with her a year ago when she took to watching golf so much. And Tiger Woods? A young black man? As far as we knew she'd never even been out of Northern Michigan, let alone seen a black person. But, it was a nice break from the incessant dinging and buzzing of game shows and the greed-driven, sex-filled soap operas that bombarded us during our visits. We accepted her love of golf though it seemed strange to see this 72-year-old polish woman watching it so intently. Her big body leaning forward. Eyes squinting. Her hand tight around a can of beer as Tiger paused at the tee. "He's beautiful. Just look at him! He'll hit it farther than anyone!"

I hear her clearing her throat over the long distance line. Then I hear her taking a drink of something. I look at my watch. It's 11 o'clock in the morning over there in her little white trailer near the lake, about the time she usually cracks her first beer of the day.

"You drinking a beer?"

"Shit no! That damned woman's got me so doped up I can't drink anything but water!"

"What woman?"

"That one from Hospice. She's a pretty little thing. And nice too. If you come home I'll introduce you."

I smile. My Grandma, sick and yellow, but trying to set me up with the woman who has come to help her die.

"She's pretty?" I ask.

"Oh yes! Dark brown hair, brown eyes, *very* pretty. Pretty like that snotty one you used to date."

"Oh, you mean Tyler?"

"Yes! That talker! I'm glad you got rid of her."

"What's this nurse's name, Grandma? Maybe I know her."

"Oh, you would have to ask…I can't remember her damned name now. Let me ask Grandpa."

She covers the phone and calls for him. I cringe.

"Sylvester! What's that nurse's name? Sylvester!"

She keeps yelling for Grandpa even though he and Uncle Dale are on the way to Posen for petunias. Mom says that since Grandma's started dying there's been more action around the trailer than ever before. Daughters cooking meals and cleaning. Sons planting flowers and trees. Grandchildren stopping by. I can't help thinking how sad and beautiful it is the way this death has awakened love.

"Oh shit," Grandma says, "I forgot. He's gone to Posen for petunias. I can't remember that nurse's name but I can find out later when she gets here. I don't remember so good anymore. It's like my brain's in pea soup."

"Do you think it's the medicine they have you on?"

"Aw shit! I'm old! That's what it is! I'm falling apart! I don't know if I should tell you this, but sometimes I piss my pants. It's embarrassing!"

Mom's told me this. That Grandma pees her pants. That my Grandma shits her pants. Sometimes she goes in her sleep and she doesn't want to get out of bed because she's afraid the mess she's made will upset everyone. Mom and Uncle Dale clean and change her and put her in her chair on the days she's too weak to do it on her own.

"Well, think of it this way," I say, "you've changed and bathed and taken care of everybody and now it's our turn to take care of you."

"It's bullshit, that's what I think. Shittin' my own pants! Can you imagine?"

I can't imagine it. Just like I can't imagine her sitting there all yellow and dying just as the best part of Michigan's Spring is coming round. The bright warming days. The cleansing rains. Grassblades and buds greening to life. Grandma is supposed to be stocking her birdfeeders and sitting near the open kitchen window watching bluejays, sparrows and canaries crack and scatter seeds. She's supposed to be doing loads of laundry and hanging the wet clothes to dry. A long wave of colors swaying in the fresh lake breeze on a line between two cedar trees. Instead, Mom goes there every day to change the bedding and make sure Grandma's clean. She loads the trunk of her car with shitty pants, pissy sheets and cries on the way home because this is not the way her Mom is supposed to be.

"You sure you don't want me to come visit?" I ask.

"Yes! I'm sure. What would you do here? Watch an old woman die?"

"Well, I have some vacation I could use and I want to see you, you know?"

Her voice is tender. "Yes. I know. I understand, but I don't want you to see me like this. Right now I'm okay and I know I'm okay, but I know that later *I* won't even know who I am." Then, her voice charges up again. "Besides, I look like a goddamned canary!"

Last time I saw her was a month ago. It was Easter time. Her trailer was decked out with bunnies, plastic eggs, and baskets overflowing with mounds of candy-filled Easter grass. She was sitting in her recliner wearing a white sweatshirt that said, "WORLD'S GREATEST GRANDMA" on it. Mom had purchased the thing at Kmart and given it to Grandma for Grandmother's Day on my behalf. Seeing her in it, knowing that she believed it was a gift from me, filled my stomach with shame.

"Wanna beer?" She asked, as I sat down in the only other chair in the room, a plastic lawn chair.

The television was on. Tiger Woods was nine under par. Grandma was glowing as she handed me a beer. But in her dimly lit trailer, I wonder, was I seeing yellow?

We cracked our beers and watched the game. Green grass. Yellow flags. Tan men in sunglasses, hats, and wrinkle-free clothes. Brand-names on everything.

"What do you think about all that advertising?" I asked.

"Oh, who cares? It's about men putting their balls into holes!"

Both of us thought about this for a moment then broke into laughter.

Grandma is not politically correct and she is not always right. What she *is* is True.

"Life's too short for bullshit!" she said to me after meeting Tyler, the girl I thought I loved—an attractive, one dimensional, vegetarian feminist who believed that it was not only ghastly in this day and age that Grandma raised and butchered chickens, hogs, and rabbits, but that it was heartless and cruel that Grandma believed that it was okay to shoot an animal if it was suffering (in this case a 13 year-old blind, arthritic hound that she asked Uncle Dale to shoot while we were visiting).

Grandma drank beer and listened to Tyler go on about animal rights, Medi-Care, and the ills of red meat. But when she started in on the harmful effects of alcohol, how it not only destroys human tissues but that its consumption is usually an indication of "deeper emotional problems", Grandma looked at me and said, "Talk! Talk! Talk! She talks too much about too many things that don't mean shit!" Then she looked at Tyler. "Do you believe in Santa Claus?"

Tyler looked at me uncomfortably. I smiled. She shifted in her chair and looked up at the fly paper hanging from the ceiling. One fly was still alive, buzzing furiously. I could tell that Tyler wanted to reach up and let it go.

"I said, DO YOU BELIEVE IN SANTA CLAUS?"

"No. I mean, I used to. When I was a kid and all, but I don't anymore."

Grandma sipped her beer. "Why not?"

"Because I think Santa is an awful form of social control."

Grandma leaned forward and smiled. Her little lips never parted, but stretched wide and made tiny dimples in her big red cheeks.

"What do you mean?" she asked.

"What I *mean* is that I would wait up for him and never see him. My Mother and Father would make me go to bed. They said that if I didn't go to bed like a good little girl Santa would not come. And they said that if I was not good and didn't go to sleep I would never grow up to be a big girl. It's a cruel hoax."

"Well then. They were right about *one* thing."

"How do you mean?" Tyler asked, her fingers locked together and white, as if praying really hard.

"Did Santa come anyway?"

"Of course. In the morning there were always presents under our tree."

"So, they were wrong about that. Santa *did* come. But look at you now. All grown up. Such a big *girl*!"

By this time the fly was screaming. Grandma leaned back and looked out the window at a sparrow that was on the window sill looking in. We could see Uncle Dale walking through the yard with a rifle in his hand.

"I mean no disrespect, Mrs. Wieschowski, but I am a *woman*, not a *girl*."

Grandma kept on looking at the sparrow. The sparrow kept on looking at her. I watched Grandma and the bird and waited for a gunshot.

Grandma, sounding bored and tired said, "I know I don't even have to ask this, but you don't believe in God, do you?"

Grandma was right. And up until then Tyler had nearly talked me into believing that God was a hoax, a trick, a crutch, that Jesus and sin were part of a story. A story created to keep all of us in line. Under control.

"Everything is not black and white, *ma'am*. There is an indefinite state of gray."

The gunshot was louder than I had expected and it made me jump in my seat. I knew then, as Tyler stood up and stomped on the floor, that we would not last.

Grandma remained in her chair and spoke quietly.

"I agree. Everything is not black and white. Everything is gray. But you are a girl and will be a girl until you start seeing and believing not only what you see, but also what you can't see."

With that, Tyler walked out the door. I looked out the kitchen window and noticed a couple of canaries had gathered near the sparrow. Uncle Dale was walking by again, this time with a shovel and a burlap sack.

Grandma stood up. "Time to feed the birds. They're waiting for me."

Having seen the size of the bag she hefted out to the porch to fill the feeders, I asked if she needed any help.

"No. You better go to your girlfriend. Things are going to be different between you now."

"Oh, I know," I said and smiled. "But thanks to you I think I'm seeing again."

Grandma turned and opened the fridge. Pickled pig's feet. Pickled herring. Hand-picked eggs. Chicken breasts thawing for supper. She reached in for a beer.

"You want one or two for the road?"

"No I better not, though I might need it to cope with her."

"Listen, she's no good for you. A talker that doesn't listen. She's got a big mouth. Not loud or obnoxious, but the size of it is big."

I was confused. "Yeah, I guess it is sort of big."

Grandma put her hand on my arm and whispered. "Girls should listen more than they talk. Everyone should. And girls with big mouths have big holes. This one, she's been around. Probably is still going around. I tell you this so you're careful."

I gave Grandma a hug, a kiss on the cheek, and told her I loved her and that I would see her again soon.

She was blushing. "Yeah, yeah, yeah. Stop with all your lovey-dovey horseshit. I got to get out there and feed the birds. The canaries are finicky and won't be back for a while if I don't get out there and feed them soon."

On the phone, I hear Grandma banging around pots and pans.
"Making lunch, Grandma?"

"Yeah, yeah, yeah. Better get ready to feed the old bastard when he gets back from Posen. If I don't he sits there like a bird on the window sill. Cheep! Cheep! Cheep! Feed me, Lucy! Feed me!"

My yellow Grandma and her yellow birds.

"Grandma, you aren't really as yellow as a canary, are you?"

"Not yet. But I will be. But that's okay. You like canaries, don't you?"

"I love canaries, Grandma."

"You don't worry and don't make the trip. There are enough of them running in and out of here all day trying to make things right again."

"Okay then, but I just want you to know…"

"Yes, I know. I know. You wanted to see me before…"

She can't say it either and I know we have to let go. That Grandma needs to rest. But I want to stay and listen to what she cannot say. Her breathing. The slight movement of the phone against her face. The polka music still there, but only slightly, like a whisper. I want to sit and talk until the phone lines go dead. To ask her to turn up the music and translate the words. To show me how to be right, even when I'm wrong, by being True.

Driving in the Rain

I had the ring, but it had been raining all day and I didn't think that's what she would want to remember. Rain. Puddles. A steady downpour of sky. I thought I'd wait to see if the sky would part and let the sun in. Besides, she seemed happy enough sitting there in the passenger seat, wearing her new fleece pullover. It was yellow, her favorite color, and 100% waterproof.

Merrill and I had been dating for two-and-a-half years. We'd met at a bar called The Stowaway during our senior year of college. It had been Oldies Night and we bumped into each other during Michael Jackson's hit song, Beat It. Some guy wearing parachute pants and a rhinestone-studded glove had dropped to the floor to do a backspin, and as I jumped back to get out of his way, I bumped into Merrill, knocking her over.

"I've fallen and I can't get up!" she yelled.

She was drunk and wearing godawful amounts of jewelry and makeup. It was hard to tell if she was Cyndi Lauper or Madonna.

I was drunk too, and shouting. "Need a lift, honey?"

"Is that you Huey Lewis?"

I stepped back and looked myself over. White blazer, pink t-shirt, white pants, no socks and white deck shoes. I had lost my mirrored sunglasses while dancing to Born in the USA.

"No Madonna! It's me! Don! Don Johnson!"

She sat up and looked at me. I reached down and took her by the arm. The dancefloor was packed with sweaty bodies spinning under flashing, colored lights.

"Don? Oh, Crockett! I'm sorry! I didn't recognize you without your sidekick, Tubbs!"

I laughed with her, but the reality of it was that Tubbs was there somewhere. Charlie Wentworth, my black neighbor from across the hall, had come up with the idea in the first place. I had been studying for a biology final when he burst into my room.

"Man! We go as Crockett and Tubbs and it's clear sailing the whole of the night! Us and the ladies is all it'll be!"

It took me a half of a case of beer to finally agree to his idea then that much more to actually get me dressed up and in line at the Stowaway.

"Great idea, Charlie," I said to him as we stood outside in the cool night air, waiting. Guys dressed as Crockett and Tubbs were everywhere.

As soon as we got in the place I lost Charlie to a young Korean girl who was dressed in a suit jacket and skirt. She had been clutching a clipboard to her chest that had CBS NEWS ANCHOR—CONNIE CHUNG written on it.

I looked around for Tubbs and Connie Chung as I lifted Merrill from the floor.

"Who you looking for? Your girl?" she asked.

"No, I was looking for Tubbs!"

"Pick one! They're everywhere!"

"Not my Tubbs!"

"You gay?"

"No! Charlie's his real name! He's my neighbor!"

She laughed and hugged me and from that moment on, we slow danced. It didn't matter that most of the songs were fast or that we were sopping wet with sweat and being bounced around by other bodies. We danced round and round. A couple of gravity-challenged fools trying to keep each other steady.

I thought of all this as we traveled down the wet highway and I marveled at the fact that since our drunken meeting we had rarely been apart. It seemed like a dream. One that you wake from but keep feeling.

A semi whooshed by and we were engulfed in a cloud of mist. I clicked the windshield wipers up a notch.

"Remember the Stowaway?" I asked.

"Do you have the headlights on?"

"Yeah, they're on."

Merrill was leafing through Cosmopolitan, sniffing perfume samples. She held a page into my face. It was a picture of young woman's tan, pierced midriff.

"You like this one?"

"It's alright, I guess."

"I'm talking about the perfume, not the girl."

"I know. It smells good. I wasn't even looking at the page. I'm trying to drive, remember?"

She closed the magazine and tossed it into the backseat. I watched a white minivan closing in behind us. A woman with wide, white eyes and a frizzy mess of hair was driving. Her hands were glued to the steering wheel at ten and two. The van was filled with kids and none of them must have been buckled up because I could see little bodies bobbing up and down in the van, playing catch with a soccerball.

The van pulled up alongside of us and a little girl in the passenger side seat stared out at us. She was holding a sign that said, *Local Union 876 Bobcats are #1*. I waved at her. She smiled and shook the sign above her head as the van zipped by.

"Think they're heading to the game, or home?" Merrill asked.

"Do they cancel soccer games on the count of rain?"

Lightning flickered through the clouds. My ears waited for the thunder, but it didn't come.

"They do if it's lightning," she said.

I remembered watching Merrill on the intramural soccer fields. Her maroon and yellow jersey. Her auburn hair pulled back into a pony tail that I liked to watch bounce and sway as she dribbled the ball. Her legs smooth, muscular, strong. After the games she'd strip down to her sports bra, and the sight of her all wet and energized was intoxicating. We both agreed that the best sex was the sex we had after her intramural games Tuesdays, Thursdays and Saturdays.

I reached over and put my hand on her thigh. Her legs were bigger than they used to be, but I had been prepared because I had seen pictures of my aunts who had played softball or basketball. Years younger, tagging runners out at second base or lining up for jump shots, their legs smooth, muscular, strong. I see these same aunts now, at family picnics or at the cottage, in shorts or bathing suits, their thick legs all bumps and veins, like they've been pelted with a ballpeen hammer.

"Are our kids going to play sports?" she asked.

"Sure. Why not?"

She put her hand on my hand. "I want a football player and a swimmer."

"I want a hockey player and a gymnast."

"That would be good. Two kids, boy or girl, it doesn't matter."

"I'd like two boys."

"You would," she said. "All you men want more men."

It was true. I thought of Merrill and I, sweaty and wet on Saturdays. Both of us locked inside each other, swallowed by the throes of post intramural sex. Fucking hard before her parents came to visit, like they did nearly every Saturday. I'd think of me, shaking hands with her tight-gripped father, feeling guilty because the hand he was holding had been on and in parts of his daughter that he never wanted any man to discover. I knew that given the opportunity, I too would want to crush the bones of the hand belonging to the man that was fucking my daughter.

I could feel the ring inside my coat rubbing my ribs as the car passed over cracks and bumps. I'd wrapped the black box with a yellow bow and placed it inside my coat like it was a living, breathing thing. I had handled it with care and thought of the insignificance of precious metals and diamonds. I had thought of how foolish we were to assign meaning to things that do not last, but knew that a few months salary was a small price to pay to show Merrill that I wanted to give her everything.

She was restless. Tapping her feet, playing with the radio, skipping through song after song.

"How long before we're there?" she asked.

We'd had entered Dakota County a mile earlier and the blue Taylor Heights water tower was now pushing up over the treetops. I was checking my sideview mirror when I noticed the ducks just ahead. In the gray mist, against the solid white line of the road, I could see two mallards. The brown one was dead, its neck broken and stretched out, one wing sticking upright. Feathers everywhere. The bright one, green and shimmering in the rain, was waiting. Head down, sitting still, feathers ruffling in gusts of car wind.

I couldn't stop. I couldn't turn around. And I knew I couldn't let Merrill see.

"What was that song you just passed?" I quickly asked. "Was that Neil Young?"

"I don't know. Which song? I've passed about a dozen."

Merrill backtracked through stations, asking me, "Was this the one?" and I watched the ducks pull away from us in the rearview mirror. The green one will die too, I thought. By starving, by crossing the road, or by being knocked silly with lead shot during duck season. An obedient lab will retrieve the bright body from a cold lake, or a stiff ground, and if the shock of it all hasn't killed the bird, the hunter will with a quick twist, a snap of the wrist.

"I can't find any Neil Young song. You sure that's what you heard?"

"Maybe it's over already. It sounded like the end, anyway."

I looked at Merrill. Her right hand was buried between her knees. She was looking out the window.

"You don't have to pee again, do you?"

"What gave it away? The clenched teeth? Tears in my eyes? The locked knees?"

"We have about half an hour to go, but there's a McDonald's up ahead if you want to stop."

"I don't know what it is. I peed twice before we left and once at that filthy rest stop. I think it's all the rain."

The golden arches were bright against the bruised sky. We parked in the lot and immediately recognized the white soccer van. As we made our way inside, we could see and hear the kids, all of them crowded at the register around the mom. I squeezed Merrill's hand.

"Looks like it'll be awhile. Go ahead and do your thing. You want a milkshake?"

"Yeah, get me a strawberry one."

I took my place in line behind the kids and waited. Everything was bright and clean. An old man wearing a burgundy McDonald's uniform was leaning on his mop, watching the children. There was one frazzled cashier, a young man about 16. He looked to the mother for help as the children shouted their orders, but her gaze was locked on the menu.

"Just give them whatever they want," she said, holding a fifty dollar bill in the air. "I've been in the car way too long with them. Burgers, fries, pop. I don't care. If it takes Ronald McDonald himself, I'll pay for it. Just give them what they want."

The old man cackled as he put away his mop and began wiping down tables. There were two women in the grill area. One was lowering a metal basket of frozen fries into a silver vat and taking drive-thru orders over her headset. The other was putting together burgers while watching a black and green computer screen. After each burger was assembled she'd drop it into its respective slot. Cheeseburger. Big Mac. Quarter pounder with cheese. I wondered how much of it these kids could eat before it all caught up with them. Before their legs, hips, and bellies all started to expand.

Merrill had returned already and I could feel her hand on my stomach.

"Maybe you ought to go for something light, like the grilled chicken sandwich," she teased.

"Very funny," I said as I sucked my gut in. "Hey, that was quick. Did you even go to the bathroom?"

"False alarm, I guess. But maybe we should eat in. I'll probably have to go again before too long."

"I thought you just wanted a shake."

"Whatever you want, but besides those candybars a while ago we haven't had anything since this morning. And it is still raining. Maybe by the time we're done eating things will clear."

"Welcome to McDonald's. May I take your order?"

The cashier's face was still red. The children had moved to the side and were circled around the mother waiting for their food. They waved their arms and chattered on and on. They looked like baby birds waiting to be fed. Merrill stepped up to order.

"I'll have the cheeseburger meal supersized, a nine piece Mcnugget, and two strawberry shakes."

"And for you sir?"

"I'll just have one of those strawberry shakes that she ordered."

"I'm not eating all that food myself!" Merrill gushed, "We'll share it!"

I recalled our stops. We had stopped at gas stations three times to pee and each time she had come back with something. Snickers bar.

Twizzlers. Doritos. A 20 ounce Pepsi or Mountain Dew. I thought of her thighs growing and growing.

    The mother had ushered the kids to a group of tables next to the playland. Some ran off to leap into a sea of plastic balls. Some jumped through holes and glided down slides. The rest dug into their food. Tiny hands shoving fries into tiny mouths by the fistfuls.
    "I don't want our kids eating crap," Merrill said as she unwrapped a cheeseburger and took a bite.
    "Me neither, but I'm sure it'll happen. Once in awhile on the way back from hockey games or swim meets."
    Merrill nodded with approval and chewed silently. She would not speak with food in her mouth and would not rest her elbows on the table. She has always had manners. Not once have I heard her chew with her mouth open, or slurp through her straw. She burps and has other bodily noises just like everyone else, but she's quick to apologize when she absolutely cannot contain them. One of the reasons she's stayed with me she's said, is because I have manners too. I'm the only person she's been able to eat with in years because it seems that everyone chews with their mouths open these days. She's told me that she can barely stand eating with her parents and that it's been this way ever since she can remember because her father is a blatant open mouth chewer. She's said that she's going to say something to him about it one day, especially before our wedding. She doesn't want him telling the video camera how much he loves us with his lips smacking and his tongue thrashing around a mouthful of food.
    We ate quietly. Both of us smiling and nodding and listening to the children near playland. The mother was talking on her cell phone letting other parents know that they'd won the game and that they were on the way home. The weather had been a bitch, she said, and some of the kids giggled. Merrill rolled her eyes and wiped her mouth in disgust. I imagined we'd never swear in front of our kids.

We got back on the road. The sun was still missing. Clouds, rain, and thunder without lightning. The gray mist was still hanging everywhere and I began to wonder if it was going to work at all.

The sun won't be there, I thought, but the bridge should still be there. And what about the bench we'd sat on? Would it be there? I had carved our initials into the wood alongside those of other lovers, but I had heard about Boy Scouts and other good-deed-doers and their desire to keep our parks clean. Raking and planting, painting and sanding. I came to the conclusion that the initials would probably be okay unless someone had started carving obscenities, then we might be in trouble.

I had planned to walk with Merrill, hand in hand, to our spot on the bridge and then ask her to marry me. Not because it was our special place, or held any particular meaning for us, but because we had both agreed that it was probably the prettiest place we'd ever been to together. I imagined us sitting on the bench fingering our wooden initials. We'd look over the edge of the bridge, into the stream, then sit awhile staring at the lake where the stream ran into it. I had remembered seeing storks standing about the shallows the time before. Tall and straight, standing on long, stick legs. They weren't storks though, Merrill had corrected me, they were Blue Herons, and they weren't waiting for babies either, they were wading for fish.

As we entered the park, I could see that things had changed. The road was paved and smaller asphalt roads trailed off into the woods in several different directions. I drove us to where I remembered the bridge to be and it was still there, but it was bigger and made of steel and concrete instead of wood. An old man wearing a blue raincoat was fishing from a wrought-iron bench.

To the right of the bridge there was a green porta-potty and by now, after the food and shake had settled, and after all of the driving in the rain, I had to go to the bathroom too.

"They've really jazzed up the place, haven't they?" I said.

"That's for sure. Doesn't even look like the same place."

"You still want to get out?" I asked.

"Would you kill me if I said no?" She clenched my hand. "I'm really not feeling well."

"It is still raining. And we can't even sit on the bridge because that guy's fishing in our spot."

"Or we can sit and wait awhile. We can watch him fish and see if leaves. I can't imagine he would sit there all day fishing in the rain."

I patted my coat pocket. The ring was still there waiting. I saw that the stream and lake were still there. The water was frothing with raindrop bubbles. It made me squirm a bit and eye the porta potty.

"Now you have to go to the bathroom, don't you?" Merrill asked with a smile.

"Yeah, and by the time I get back, I'm sure you'll have to go again too."

Out of the car, through puddles. The air was fresh and I sucked as much of it as I could into my lungs because I couldn't ever remember rain smelling so good. Wet pines, wet grass, wet ground. Birds muffled through wet leaves and boughs. I heard the old man coughing from his place on the bridge. I watched him bait his hook until he looked my way. I smiled, but I imagined he couldn't see me because we were too far away from each other. I thought of how lonely he must be to go out and fish off a park bridge in the rain.

The porta potty stunk like shit and stale water. I tried not to look down into the hole while I was pissing, but I couldn't help myself. Tampons, beer bottles, and diapers. Everything that didn't belong there was there mixed with shit. I looked at the sign that said, "PLEASE DO NOT DEPOSIT GARBAGE INTO THE TOILET" and was thankful that it had been raining all day because maybe it was helping to keep the stench down.

I stepped out into the rain and breathed deep again. Merrill was sitting in the car looking ahead at the old man, or the bridge, or at something else I could not see. I noticed for the first time that she'd picked up a double chin somewhere along the way. I felt something stir inside of me, like fright and excitement, like being chilled from the inside out, but it came and went so quickly that I wondered if I'd felt it at all. For an instant, I felt I knew something, but I wasn't sure what it was. I looked in the direction that Merrill was looking until I got to the car.

"What are you looking at?"

"Us. I'm remembering us on the bridge."

"That was a good day, wasn't it?"

"Yes. We've come far, haven't we?"

"But it seems like yesterday."

I felt for the ring in my pocket and leaned toward Merrill. I caught a glimpse of myself in the rearview mirror and noticed something different—my very own double chin. I felt my belt tighten against my stomach as I kissed her cheek and imagined that it was probably time to move up another notch. Her skin was soft and familiar against my lips. Rain or not, sun or clouds, growing thighs or double chins, what did any of it matter? We were together and time would change us by keeping us the same.

"It's not just having a full bladder," she said.

"What are you talking about?"

"And I know you've noticed the weight gain."

I sat back in my seat and stared at the man on the bridge. He was unhooking a flip-flopping sunfish from his line. When I saw the fish's yellow belly, I thought of Merrill and I on the bridge that day I had carved our initials into wood. I wondered if anyone had been watching us. From the parking lot, or from the woods. Maybe with binoculars from across the lake. What were they thinking as we leaned over the bridge and looked into the water? Did they know that we were watching perch minnows, dark and gray against a bright stream bottom? If they had seen us, they couldn't have known what we did—that someone had thrown red and blue aquarium rocks into the water. That the perch minnows seemed to like it there hovering above the colors like people staring at a painting trying to decipher texture, pattern, meaning. I wondered if a family had put a pet fish to rest, if they had carried the whole aquarium there not knowing that it had died from some fish disease. Maybe the perch minnows had succumbed to the disease and maybe it had infected the stream. Beyond the lake, I wondered where the stream would lead.

I turned my attention back to Merrill. Her eyes looked sad.

"I've gained some weight too," I said, "All I do lately is eat. We just need to get outside and exercise more."

"But you're not pregnant," she said.

I had heard her say it, but it was still deep inside of me, moving around in my veins with the aquarium gravel, the old man on the bridge and the ducks on the side of the road. I wondered if on our way home we'd see the ducks again. I imagined the green one would still be there. It wouldn't leave. Not the way it had been sitting there with its head buried in its breast, body shaking from tons of metal passing only feet away. It would die too and would not see another duck season. It would never see the flash of gunshot or the blackness of a splashing lab, and it would never feel the water change into anything besides what it had always been, something familiar and true, like lifeblood. Everything started to make sense as the rain dwindled to sprinkles

Her voice was shaking. "Did you hear what I said?"

The old man had packed up and left our place on the bridge.

"I heard you just fine," I said. "Let's go outside and talk. The rain's letting up and I'd like to be by the stream."

As we got out of the car, I could feel her uncertainty. I breathed the rainy air and stretched and yawned. I could feel the blood rushing up through me and felt like I could run for miles. I took the ring from my pocket and clutched it in my hand as Merrill and I danced around the puddles.

Flag Day

In a stinking bar—ashtrays and cigarettes, hands holding dirty glasses, puddles of beer on the floor and on the table, the jukebox pounding the stale sweaty air—but, I can smell her. Just showered, Ivory skin. Clean, strawberry smelling hair. Our elbows touching and energy shooting from pore to pore, rifling through our layers, pushing deep inside to places that feel familiar because it feels like they've never been touched before.

We sit with co-workers at four long tables that have been joined together to celebrate. Tommy is leaving. The six foot six hunk of business man, who makes more than most of us combined, is leaving us to be an executive for Ford Motor Company in Battle Creek. All I know about Battle Creek is that they make cereal there.

The people surrounding the table are misfits like me. College graduates who work because we need to so that we can do what we love. At the table I'm at there's a guitar player, an artist, and the sculptor, Eileen. She, like the rest of us, has been working at Cheney's Design Inc. for a year-and-a-half because that's how long the company's been around. We came aboard because of promises. Two weeks of vacation, 401k, a casual dress code, and the possibility of stock options.

Tommy had said that coming in on the ground floor of a new company meant one thing—that all of us would be moving up. So far, he's the only one to go, and he's been running the company. I wonder about the loyalty and dedication that Tommy spoke of when he recruited us, and even though I think he's a heartless asshole, I'm sad to see he's leaving because we need people like him to run companies while the rest of us are running the world.

I can't believe how good Eileen smells in all of this. Her scent grounds me and as our legs find each other under the table, I keep fighting myself. She's married, I think. Married and has a kid. I can't decide what it is about her that gets me, but something does. It isn't her body, I think, because frankly she's bigger than any other girl I've ever liked. So maybe it's her long blonde hair and the way her bangs curl and sweep down in front of her eyes. She looks at me a lot through that wispy hair and she knows that her blue eyes are an advantage. If she works at it, like she usually does, we'll end up calling a cab and heading to my apartment. From there, she'll call her husband.

"I'm staying in the city tonight," she'll say, "because I'm too drunk to drive. Make sure you get up early enough to get Billy off to school."

I'll watch her talk and lie and I'll wonder at the foolishness of trust, the boundaries of vows and commitment, but I soon forget them because those are things that do not belong to me. And when the phone's back in its cradle, we'll go right to it. We'll be up and down and all around the apartment, from room to room, chair to floor, carpet to linoleum. When it's all over I'll feel like shit because I can't feel as good as I want to knowing that everything we've just done might be solidifying two advanced tickets to hell. Everything goes away in the darkness though, when she snuggles up and drapes her arms around me, when I feel her breathing.

I'm talking to Chuck, the guitar player, about Hemingway and fishing when Eileen puts her head on my shoulder.

I say to her, like I always do, "People are going to start talking, you know." And she whispers in my ear, "I don't care."

"You guys aren't hiding anything," Chuck says, "It's obvious you two have been fucking for a while now."

The free beer, courtesy of the cigar-puffing, suit-wearing Tommy, is starting to kick in. Some have heard what Chuck's said, but thankfully Tommy's busy running his mouth about the Mercedes he's going to buy so not everyone has heard.

I lean over the table toward Chuck.

"Jesus Christ. You want to get us fired?"

The artist, Jennifer, has two cents to put in. "Fired for what? For taking some pleasure in this miserable fucking world? This goddamned company...they ought to give everyone a fucking sex slave as a bonus. Wasn't that in our contract?"

We laugh and drink and pour more beer. I see a light come on in the apartment across the street. There's a woman pacing back and forth in front of the window talking on a telephone. She's wearing a white robe and has a towel on her head. The woman has a nice dark tan, or she might be Mexican. I think about the word Mexican and I wonder if there's a word that's more politically correct. It's hard to tell with all the rightness in the world. All I know for sure is that she's very attractive from what I can see of her. I look for a wedding ring shining through the window glass, or for photographs of children on the wall.

"Hemingway could kick Tommy's ass," Chuck says.

Chuck's an African American, but he's told me it's okay to call him black even though he's a brown chubby man. He's been playing guitar since he was eight years old. He's attended Interlochen, made and sold his own CDs, and plays on Saturdays at the Music Cafe down the street.

"Tommy's pretty big..." I begin to say, but Jennifer jumps in.

"Before you two start talking about Hemingway and all the asses he could kick, I have something that I've been wanting to ask you, Chuck."

"Sure, go ahead."

"It's of a personal nature."

"Nothing's personal anymore. You know that."

"Okay then. My question is this…In this world of so-called equality I still think that the reason I haven't made it yet is because I'm a woman. Do you think that the reason you haven't made it yet is because you're an African American?"

"Because I'm black? That's bullshit. I'm making it now. And so are you. To hell with all that. What is making it? Is being like Tommy making it? Because if so, I don't want any part of it. Look at him…what an asshole! Not only could Hemingway kick his ass, I think he would do it for fun!"

Miraculously, there's a moment of silence in the bar. The jukebox is changing songs, conversation has lulled, and Tommy's heard what Chuck has said about Hemingway kicking his ass.

"You talking about that fucking writer?"

"You can read, Tommy?" Jennifer yells. Everyone laughs.

"Fuck all of you! I could kick any writer's ass!"

"Not Hemingway." I say, and there's more laughter.

Tommy stands up and smiles.

"That's right. You're a writer, aren't you?"

I nod my head and sip my beer. I see that the woman from the lighted apartment is gone. I think maybe she's getting dressed to go out and think that it's too bad her bedroom window isn't facing the bar because it would really drum up business. I feel Eileen's hand on my arm. I can tell she doesn't want me to start anything with Tommy because she knows I won't back down.

My silence and the laughter of others has hurt Tommy. He's getting red in the face and I notice that his big hands are clenched into fists.

"Don't worry about it, Tommy. Hemingway's dead."

"Because someone like me probably kicked his ass!"

"Yeah, it actually was something like that," I say.

Across the street, the woman is in her window. She's on the phone again, wearing a black bra and unraveling the towel from around her head. She's bent over to let it all out and for a second I lose sight of her. When she pops up again I feel warm. From the beer, from Tommy's bullshit, and from the sight of her with that long dark hair.

"A toast!" Chuck yells, "To Tommy and to Flag Day!"

"Flag Day?" Tommy says, "Fuck that! To Tommy! And it's no wonder I'm leaving after working with a bunch of freaks and queers for so long! You fuckers really weird me out the way you talk about queer shit all the time. Maybe you are all queer, but it doesn't matter. Let the queers sing their songs, write their stories, and play with clay. In a month I'll be driving by in my new Mercedes and if you're lucky I'll slow down long enough to wave!"

Everyone laughs and drinks. I turn and look at Chuck.

"Is it really Flag Day?"

"I guess so. I got up to mark yesterday off on the calendar and it said June fourteenth—Flag Day. I thought it would be best to change the subject. Tommy's loaded."

"Yeah, but Hemingway could still kick his ass."

Eileen pushes her body against mine.

"We ought to go soon," she says.

"What do you mean? The beer's on Tommy and we're just getting started."

"I know but I'm tired."

I think about the woman in her lighted apartment, slipping a white blouse over her black bra. I imagine she's probably in the bathroom, finishing up her hair, spreading on scented body lotion for someone to inhale.

"Can we hang just a little while longer? I like talking about this shit."

"What shit?"

"Hemingway and stuff."

She rolls her eyes and smiles.

"You boys and your talk. Hemingway's dead and his time is up. He's out and Nicholas Sparks is in. But I don't want to get into this.

Maybe Tommy's right. Maybe you boys are a little queer. Do you really like each other?"

"We love each other!" Chuck shouts as he raises his glass.

All of us clink glasses, except Eileen. She gets up and goes to the bathroom. I imagine that when she gets back it'll be time to go.

"You two are fucking, aren't you?" Jennifer asks.

"Leave him alone!" Chuck says.

"Why should I?"

"Because you're just jealous because he's giving her cock and not you!"

"I don't like cock, remember?"

We forget sometimes that Jennifer is a lesbian because she is amazingly beautiful. She is a tall, shapely, red-head. Besides being an artist, she's a lifeguard and she runs in marathons. The woman is a glorious physical specimen.

"That's what I mean! You want to be the one giving it to her!"

Chuck is laughing, Jennifer pauses to sip her drink and I can tell she's thinking of something to say. It's a nice break in the action because I like the way her lips touch the glass.

"Very funny, Charlie, but I'm afraid she's not even worthy of my dildo."

Chuck laughs again, and so do I because all of us are getting drunk and I'm thinking that if Hemingway was alive I bet he wouldn't mind being right here with us. Drinking, laughing, and talking shit—especially on Flag Day.

Tommy's drinking shots. There's a busty waitress making him keep his hands off her and the glass. He's told he has to keep his head tilted back and remain still so that she can pour the shot down his throat. Tommy tells her that he'll sit still if she pours the drink from her tits. He says that there's a big tip in it for her, so the girl straddles him, puts the shot glass between her tits and pours it down his throat beautifully. It doesn't look like it could be done better in a movie.

Tommy starts gagging on the stuff and then he starts swearing. He stuffs a five dollar bill into the waitress' cleavage, then wanders off in the direction of the bathroom.

"I hope he pukes his guts out," Jennifer says.

"Do you think Hemingway puked?" Chuck asks.

"Sure. That's how you build stamina, isn't it?" I ask.

"You two shouldn't idolize Hemingway so much," Jennifer says.

"Sure we should. We're in our twenties. Isn't that right, Chuck?"

"In our time that's what we need. We need another Hemingway."

I fill all of our glasses, including Eileen's, in hopes that when she's done doing whatever she'll want to sit and drink some more. I glance at the apartment window across the street and the light is off. The woman is gone.

"I don't know why we talk about him like we do," I say. "I like his writing because it's about fishing and natural things. It's where we belong."

"I think you boys love him because he's a symbol of masculinity and because it makes you feel tough. I mean, do you really think he could survive in our world today?"

"No." I say, "He isn't a symbol and he couldn't live in our time. We don't give a shit about anything but making money, buying things, and creating walls to call home. We're a bunch of soulless assholes. Look at us. The only reason we're here is too drink for free. We sit and bitch about the weight of a politically correct world and all I really want to do is get drunk, go home, fuck, and fall asleep."

"That's good to know," Eileen says, as she comes up from behind and puts her arms around me.

Jennifer drains her beer then gets up to leave. "Okay kids. The shit's getting deep, so I think I'll be going. I'm supposed to go running tomorrow morning."

Chuck stands and stretches. "Yeah, I better get moving too. I have to be at the Cafe early tomorrow to set up. You guys coming down to listen?"

We tell him that we'll be there because we will. We have to stick together in all of this because there aren't many of us left. If there are, they're silent and living alone in apartments across the street from bars. They're coming home late from work, dressing up, putting on something new, so that they can go out and dance, and drink, and look for something that's missing so they'll have meaning.

Eileen sits down next to me and begins to drink. "Maybe I should go home tonight. You know?"

I wonder what happened in the bathroom to change her mind. If it is Flag Day and the fourteenth of June, I know her period's about two weeks away.

The empty glass is warm in my hand and I am full. I think about Eileen driving home to her husband and getting into bed with him. I wonder if he snuggles up to her when she comes home, or if she snuggles up to him. Does he smell all that she's done? The beer, the smoke, the infidelity?

Outside the window, the woman from the apartment is walking across the street. Under the lights, in her white blouse and black skirt, she's looking like some Dark Lady Shakespeare would write about. When she reaches our side of the street, a man on a bicycle nearly plows into her. He has a long, scraggly beard and is wearing a backpack against his naked skin. Sticking out of the pack, wavering through the night air, is an American Flag. The woman is shocked and scared, and in an instant dictated by nothing but invisible fate, our eyes meet through the window glass. I can see she's rethinking everything.

"Yeah, maybe sleeping alone will be good," I say to Eileen as I take another drink.

I hear the door open and some of the bar goes out into the night. I wonder if the shirtless man with the flag has heard anything. I wonder if anyone else along the street outside is awake. If they are, what are they doing? Are they drinking? Watching television? Surfing the Internet? Does anyone read anymore?

Eileen eyes the Dark Lady as she walks into the bar and looks at me.

Eileen fidgets in her chair, "I could stay a little while longer," she says.

"No, that's alright. I want to get out of here before Tommy gets back from the bathroom anyway. I don't even want to say goodbye to that sonofabitch."

All of us walk out together, through smoke, music and laughter. I watch the Dark Lady take a stool at the bar and by the way she moves and sits I can tell she's someplace familiar. I catch sight of Tommy coming out of the darkness. He's wiping his mouth. He's making his way to the bar. I know that once I'm outside, if I turn around, he'll be at her side promising to buy the next round.

The Drive

Since Mom's death five years ago Dad's stopped going to church. Instead, he calls me Saturday nights to confirm our trips for Sunday. When I'm not there he talks to my machine.

"Jim, this is Dad. Just called to shoot the shit. Guess you're not home so I'll see you tomorrow...bout six-thirty then."

His voice is deep and mechanical. He doesn't have a good phone voice, a good answering machine voice. Mom's the one that used to have the good voice. The one that did all the talking. Dad used to call her chatter-box. All I have left of Mom's voice is in my memory. Dad's is on tape. I have a shoebox of answering machine tapes filled with Dad's messages. They're all about the same but I save them anyway.

Every Sunday I wake up at six o'clock in the morning to make the half hour drive to Dad's house. When I get there he's always sitting at the kitchen table drinking black coffee, flipping through the pages of *Field & Stream*. Today though, when I walk into his house at six thirty, he isn't sitting there. I call through the house and there's no answer so I walk down the hallway toward his room.

The walls are plastered with photographs of the family because up until Mom died we had a picture taken every year. Me, Mom and Dad—the three of us together, always seated in the same pose. Mom and Dad sitting facing each other, holding hands. Me standing in the middle behind them. My face is younger and thinner. My hair is thicker and black. I don't look at the pictures anymore. The walls are invisible to me. I've seen them enough to know that what hangs in the hallway is it. Family framed in wood and metal. Memories preserved behind sheets of glass.

    I stand outside Dad's bedroom for five minutes. I'm frozen to the floor, afraid to open the door because I start thinking about the day I found Mom. How I came in the house calling her name and there was no answer. How I walked down the hallway and stopped outside the bathroom door. I called her name. I knocked. There was no sound of her at all. When I opened the door, she was on the bathroom floor with her pants around her ankles. Her eyes were open, but seeing nothing. Her skin so blue it looked black.

    I touch the doorknob of Dad's room and think about leaving. I think about going home, but I know that chances are when I get there, there'll be a message on the machine from Dad. He'll be wondering where the hell I'm at.

    I turn the knob and when the door opens I see him. He's curled up in bed, wearing red pajamas. I step over a tangled mess of sheets and blankets, go to his bed and sit down. He doesn't move. His mouth is wide open though, air whistling in and out. Seeing him breathe makes me feel better. His face is loose and relaxed. Wrinkles I've never noticed before are everywhere. Mom used to make him pluck his eyebrows, but he doesn't anymore so he's got this long bushy caterpillar above his eyes. I want to touch his face because I can't ever remember doing it, but I don't. Instead, I stand up and give the room the once over.

    He's got the spittoon he bought ten years ago sitting on the floor next to his bed. It's silver, about two feet tall, and shaped like an hourglass. The sides are engraved with thin lines that create a wildlife scene. A whitetail buck drinking from a pond.

    I remember Dad bringing the spittoon home from his fishing trip to Canada. He said he got it for a song from a souvenir shop just this side of the Mackinaw Bridge. And I remember Mom swearing to God that she'd never allow him to have such a disgusting object in her house, not while she was alive. Dad told her he didn't plan on using it to spit in. Instead, he planned to use it for spare change. I look inside the spittoon and I can tell it isn't holding any pennies, nickels or dimes. There's a line of dried tobacco spit stretched down the side.

Dad's got a Bible on his nightstand and I'm not sure why. He's never been much into religion. Mom had to bribe him into church with Sunday suppers of scalloped potatoes and evening drives through the countryside. I wonder what passages he's been reading so I pick up the book. There's a *Buck's Bait and Tackle* receipt serving as a bookmark. I open to the page that's marked and see that Dad's got a part of Psalm 6 underlined in pencil.

Have mercy on me, O LORD, for I am weak; O LORD, heal me, for my bones are troubled.

Further down, he's got another part underlined, this time in pen.

I am weary with my groaning; all night I make my bed swim; I drench my couch with my tears.

Dad lets out a sigh and I turn to look at him. He's curled up tighter now, his chin nearly meeting his knees. I set the Bible back on the nightstand. I look to his alarm clock for the time and notice that the hands have stopped. Time is dead. I pick up the clock and head to the kitchen for batteries because Dad keeps everything in the kitchen. Next to spices and crackers is fishing line and 3-in-one oil. The breadbox holds nuts and bolts, shotgun shells and batteries. As I step out of the room, I hear Dad rustling around, his throat gurgling. I'm in the hallway with his dead clock in my hands when he wakes.

"Christ, if ya don't wanna go for a ride with your old man, just tell him, don't steal his damned clock."

I tell him the batteries are dead and that I'm going to put new ones in. He stands and pulls a pair of jeans on over his pajamas. He takes the clock from my hand and says he knows the batteries are dead. He puts the clock on the nightstand next to the Bible and tells me that he's been in bed wondering when the hell I was going to show up. I'm right on time as usual, but I apologize for being late.

"I'll make coffee," I say.

"We're going to Male's Store, we'll get something there."

"You gonna wear pajamas under your clothes?"

"Always do. Go warm up the truck."

I walk out of the house thinking of Dad, wondering if he's really worn pajamas under his clothes all these years. If he has, I wonder how I've gone for so long without knowing.

I get in the truck and stare at the blue Ford emblem on the steering wheel. The truck is seven years old. The inside smells like salt-and-vinegar chips and Copenhagen. But beneath it, I can still smell the newness of plastic dashboard parts and vinyl seats. The smell the truck had when Dad had a spring in his step, I had hair on my head, and Mom was alive.

Dad emerges from the house with binoculars dangling around his neck. He's wearing khakis, a red flannel shirt, and an old pair of Rocky boots—the same boots Mom got him the Christmas before she died. He walks around to the passenger side of the truck, slips, and nearly falls. When he boosts himself into the truck he's breathing pretty heavy.

"You all right?" I ask.

"Goddamned boots are bald."

"Time for a new pair, hey?"

"Nah, I'll have em' resoled."

Dad reaches into his shirt pocket and takes out his Copenhagen. He opens it and the rich smell wafts into the cab. He takes a pinch and some of it sprinkles onto his shirt. He places the dip inside his lip, closes the can and puts it back into his pocket. As he brushes away the black sprinkles, I notice his belly's gotten bigger. I suck in my own gut and sit up straight. Dad reaches under his seat and brings up a plastic Coke bottle. It's half full of chunky brown liquid. He unscrews the cap, holds the bottle to his lips and adds to the murky brown. As I back the truck out onto the road, Dad crams the bottle between his legs for safekeeping then begins cleaning the binocular lenses with his shirttail.

It's early October and the leaves are bleeding away. Some have dried up, like rotten fruit and fallen to the ground. There's just enough breeze to send some of them swirling around. The fields are grayish brown and spotted with lumpy round hay bales. Cows are standing and horses are walking, all of them oblivious to us as we drive by. Their big glossy eyes are baring into the ground.

As we near Male's Corner Store, Dad spits into the Coke bottle again, then asks me a question.

"You know why they call it Male's Corner?"

"Because the guy who owns the store is named Male?"

"You ever hear what your Mom thought?"

"No, what?"

"Years ago there was these two young kids just outta high school that decided to get married. It was December twenty-third, two days before Christmas, and I remember we weren't having much of a winter. In fact, when the call came in, I was raking the yard."

"When the call came in?"

"Yeah, I was a volunteer firefighter for a while."

"You were?"

"Yep, up until you came along. Then there wasn't time for me to be running around taking care of other people when I had my hands full with you and Mom."

"I never knew you were a firefighter."

"I never told you?"

"Not that I remember."

"Well I was and I remember your mother complaining about the gravel that had been pushed off the road into our yard by the plow trucks. Since it was the holidays, we were having the usual Christmas company, relatives that I don't care to see, and your mother was worried that they'd see the rocks in the lawn. I told her it was winter for

God's sake, and it didn't matter a whole hell of a lot what the yard looked like. I mean we were having these people in our house for Crissakes! Feeding them, talking to them, playing cards and all that happy horseshit. It's not like they were gonna be walking barefoot in the lawn or some goddamned thing."

"Sounds like Mom all right. Always worried about what everyone thinks."

"No shit. So anyway, I end up out there, day before Christmas Eve, trying to rake rocks out of a frozen lawn. To top it off, we ended up getting enough snow that day to keep the ground covered for three months. The shit just kept coming and coming. But it wasn't the snow that did them kids in. What did them kids in was what they couldn't see."

"A whiteout?"

"Nope. Black ice."

"That's not good."

"Nope. The group of them were heading to Long Rapids Chapel for the ceremony. The bride and her girlfriends were in one car, the groom and his boys were in another. The boys were following the girls and both cars were driving pretty fast. I guess they were playing around you know, the girls trying to keep the bride out of sight, the old bad luck tradition.

"Anyhow, there's that sharp corner just before you get to that bridge you know, but apparently the girls didn't slow down. Had they hit that ice going the speed limit, the guardrail might have saved them. But they were really trucking along, probably really excited trying to get to the church and all. When I got there, there were all these boys, dressed up in tuxedos on the bridge. The groom, he was hanging over the edge of the railing where the car had went over into the river. He was screaming and crying and two of his boys were holding him back. So he wouldn't jump over, I guess. It was like a bad dream. All those people dressed up, on their way to a wedding, but ending up there on the bridge watching the bride and her girlfriends sink into the river."

"Nobody survived?"

"The men did. The car they were in bounced off the guardrail and spun into the center of the road. The girls though, they all died. One girl wasn't found till Spring."

"Jesus Christ, Dad. What did you tell me that for?"

"That's why your Mom thought they called it Male's Corner! Because all the men survived!"

"Male's store wasn't there?"

"Nope. That wasn't built till the following year."

"You would think he would have named it something else."

"What for?"

"Because of what happened to the girls."

"But Male's his goddamned name!"

"Yeah, but out of respect for the families."

"Aw, bullshit."

"Well, it's an eerie coincidence, anyway."

"No, it's an eerie story is all. Worse things have happened."

When we get to the corner, where the bridge is, I slow to a crawl because the turn into the store's lot is tight and because I'm trying to see something, to see anything that would make the story real. Marks on the pavement. A repaired guardrail. But there isn't anything. Too much time has passed for there to be anything. An empty beer can rolls around with some leaves.

The tank isn't empty when we pull into Male's Corner. The gauge is on the edge of full, but Dad says he wants it filled anyway. He ambles into the store while I pump gas. The pump's old as hell with rolling black and white digits, and even though I can barely squeeze in two dollar's worth, it takes about five minutes. I gaze at the bridge and can hear the river moving along restlessly, eroding as much of the bank as it can before its course is slowed by ice floats and frozen debris. Though the sun is rising above the naked hardwood trees, it's barely visible. A veil of murky white sky is moving in. When I remove the nozzle from the filler tube it's dripping with gasoline. Some of it splashes onto my shoes. I put the nozzle back into the pump and look at my feet. They're the same shoes Mom got me in 93', around Easter time. The spots of gasoline disappear, some evaporating, some seeping into my shoes. I think maybe it's time I get a new pair.

I hear Dad and Mr. Male inside the store laughing, carrying on as usual. Although their conversation appears light, as soon as I walk in they're silent, as though they've been discussing something of utmost seriousness. Mr. Male's face is tight and fresh, his lips parted into a smirk. He has a shiny, spotted, bald head. The only thing I've ever heard him say in my presence is our total for the day.

"Tree nineynine with your gas."

It's always the same and his voice gives nothing away. It's just a plain declarative voice. No cracking, no depth or height to it. No life.

Dad's got our bounty spread out on the counter in front him. Two bottles of Coke and a big bag of salt-and-vinegar chips. The cash register clings and chings, like bells singing, as Mr. Male pushes the clicking digits. When the total springs up Mr. Male nods at me then winks at Dad, "Tree nineynine, with your gas," he says.

Dad tells him that we don't need a bag, then scoops the goodies up into his arms. He hands me the Cokes, tells me not to shake them, and I realize that I've never learned Mr. Male's first name. The man with the spotted, bald head, who forever charges "tree nineynine" is nameless.

When we get to the truck I ask, "Dad, what's his first name?"

"Whose first name?"

"Mr. Male's."

Dad stops and looks back at the store. "Hell if I know, but he said he saw a big buck just the other side of Mustang Swamp this morning."

"We ought to check it out then, hey?"

"Yep. We ought to."

We get into the Ford with the tank full up and our goodies in hand. Dad spits out his chew and tears into the chips. He takes a handful then sets the bag between us on the seat. He munches away, crumbs falling onto his shirt and all around him. His eyes seem to be fixed on the window glass rather than the scenery on the other side. By the time we're on the road and have been moving for three miles or so, the chips have taken their toll. Our Cokes are half gone and we both have to pee. As usual, we decide to go at Smith's Totem Pole.

The pole sits off the road a ways, just the other side of the ditch. We call it Smith's Totem Pole because the closest mailbox to it has SMITH painted on it. The pole's been standing there on the road for as long as I can remember. It's about fifteen feet tall and is all wooden animals. It's only big enough to disguise one body at a time standing sideways, but we go there anyway. When Dad goes, I see a leak spring out of the ear of a raccoon. When I go, Dad says that he sees pee squirting out from the skunk's tail.

Once we're empty and refreshed, when we've stretched out the last heavy bit of morning, we settle into our ride. We move slowly, at about ten miles an hour, down County Road 451. It's an old dirt road that begins at Male's Corner and circles Valley View Township. It's a long gravelly-dirt stretch that's all stone farmhouses and hunting camps. Places you can't see from the road because of long winding driveways or fenced-in yards guarded by trees.

As we drive past a few off-roads, trails really, Dad pulls his gaze from the window and looks at me.

"Years ago your Mom and I used to run these roads."

The Ford jumps over a few potholes and shakes us. I want to say something, but I don't know what or how. Dad pauses, as if searching for the right moment of memory, then continues.

"We used to hop into my old Chrysler, grab a case of Blatz from Male's and just go ridin'. There's nice quiet places at the end of those trails."

"What did you do back there?" I ask.

Dad smiles and says, "We'd just sit and talk."

"Sure, Dad." I tease, "I've been down some of those trails myself."

"I know ya have! Bending curfews with Emily Thompson!"

"What are you talking about?"

I look at him and his smile shoots warmth into my gut. I feel excited and caught, like a kid again.

Dad laughs, "You may've fooled Mom, but not me."

My face burns red, my hands are moist on the steering wheel.

"That was my car you borrowed those nights," he continues, "Comin' back with mud and grass all underneath. Beer cans jammed under the seat."

We laugh and I remember driving those trails. Barely passable wooded two tracks, grassy and deep, that led to wide open fields and thick swamps. Places where people dumped bulging, black garbage bags, unwanted furniture, and old washing machines. Me and Emily Thompson in Dad's car, drinking beer and getting farther along with each empty can.

The only traffic we see on our Sunday drive is the Donakowski family on their way to church. They pass us at Mustang Swamp, the lowest part of the road where the cedar trees loom over and envelop us in thick heavy shade. They whiz by waving, their Chevy Suburban tossing gravel. Dad shakes his head and calls them assholes for driving so goddamned fast, on a Sunday of all days. He shifts his attention to the window again, this time moving his head around, taking everything in. I wonder if he's thinking about the sky, that there really isn't one today. That there are only flashes of light that manage to steal a way through the cloud cover and the cracks in the only green that remains, that of the pines and cedars.

We roll up alongside a wide sprawling field. We don't know for sure who owns this property. We've never known. Dad tells me that he's heard it's a guy from Bloomington Hills that comes up with a bunch of his GM buddies. That they've got a camp back in the woods somewhere that sits on a ridge which divides the cedar swamp from the hardwoods. They've got a bar, a sauna, and two pool tables. That's what Mr. Male's told him, he says.

Dad motions for me to stop. He gets out his Copenhagen and takes another dip. There's a volcano-shaped rock pile in the center of the field. I can see some deer standing about a hundred yards out. Dad raises the binoculars to his brow and I watch him as he tries to find the deer in the binoculars. The time it takes him to scan the field is longer nowadays. His hair is salt-and-pepper gray. He seems shorter and smaller, but maybe that's because his posture isn't as good as it used to be. I sit up straight and keep watching. His cheeks are heavier, sagging—gravity seems to be winning. He adjusts the focus knob and his hands are shaking.

"Two Does, one looks like a yearling."

He hands the binoculars to me. I can't see a thing the way he's adjusted the lenses, so I adjust them to my eyes. I see the Does, but I also see something else. A gray, thick-shouldered eight-point buck standing next to them.

Dad lifts his Coke to his lips, unscrews the cap, and instead of taking a drink, spits into it. He puts the cap on and realizes what he's done.

"For Crissakes, I just spit in my pop."

"You can have my pop if you want it."

I hand him the binoculars.

Dad raises the glasses to his eyes, adjusts the lenses and takes another look. I grip the wheel and bite my tongue. I hold my breath in silence and wait. He turns away from the window and hands the binoculars back to me. His hands are steady now and look strong. I wonder if he sees it. I want him to see it because that's what we're looking for. I want to hear Dad say that he sees it, that it's all muscles and antlers, and that the reason its coat is gray is because we're in for an early winter.

"You better take another look," he says.

"Did you see it?" I ask.

He says yes, but I'm not sure he has. I put the binoculars to my eyes, adjust them and see nothing. The field is gray and brown, stiffened grasstips waver in the wind. I see a crow fly into view and land on the rock pile. I see the hardwoods in the distance, naked on top, with the few colors that remain bleeding against the gray sky. But the deer are gone.

A Better Place

Bill gave in on his own terms. He rattled the cage, killed the bird, then gave the feathers to his daughter, Sally.

"Where's Sonny?" Sally asked.

"In a better place," Bill answered.

"Will he come back?"

Bill touched her face and put the feathers in her hair. She reddened with excitement and began to dance.

"You'll see him again, I promise."

"Sonny's in a better place! Sonny's in a better place! And I'm going to see him!"

He had taken the cage outside to the dumpster in the alley and thrown the whole thing, bird and all, away.

Bill was at the table mixing beer and tomato juice when Marie came home from work.

"Where's the bird? I see feathers in my daughter's hair, but I don't see a cage and I don't see a bird."

Bill swirled the red round and round with a spoon. The clinking of metal against glass sounded like bells underwater.

"And why are you drinking already? I wish you'd wait until after supper."

"I can't drink it straight anymore. It hurts."

"You're tearing your insides up again."

She put her briefcase on the table then began rubbing Bill's shoulders. He sipped the drink then added some salt.

"Marie, I'm sorry. But it wouldn't stop chirping. Sally was in her room playing Barbie or some goddamned thing and the fucking bird wouldn't stop."

"Do you just let her alone all day?"

"No, my imaginary friend, Bruce, plays with her."

"When are we gonna eat?" Sally called from the livingroom.

Marie stopped rubbing Bill's shoulders. She walked to the refrigerator and took out a chicken. Bill gulped down his bloody beer and chuckled.

"I killed the kid's bird, and you're making chicken. That's kinda funny."

Marie tossed the bird onto the counter.

"It's not funny, Bill. Are you losing your mind?"

"It doesn't matter. She doesn't know. I gave her the feathers and told her that old Sonny's in a better place."

Marie sat down across from Bill.

"Did you call on any jobs today?"

"Two."

"And that did they say?"

"They took my name and number and said they'd be in touch."

"That's it?"

"Yes, that's it. What can I say?"

"You can tell me that you'll go and get your old job back."

"I don't want my old job back."

"But you have to work. I can't do this on my own. It's bad for me knowing that you and Sally are here alone all day. I keep thinking that you'll drink yourself to death and Sally will wander off and get lost."

Bill got up and stretched. He walked to the refrigerator and looked inside.

"Did you at least write anything today?" Marie asked.

"I wrote a poem."
"Can I read it?"
"No. It's in the early stages."
"Well can I at least read what you do have?"
"That'd be difficult."
"How come?"
"It's in my head, that's why. Like I said, it's in the early stages."
"Words in your head aren't paying the bills."
Bill closed the refrigerator.
"I got to go to the store."
"You're losing us, Bill."
"I know. I'm losing me too."
Marie walked over to Bill.
"Honey, you look awful. What's happening to you? You're not the same Billy anymore."
"Billy's okay, it's *me* I'm worried about."
"When are we gonna eat?" Sally called again.
"As soon as Daddy gets back from the store, baby."
Marie leaned into Bill and kissed his bristly face.
"Don't you even shave anymore?"
"Just my legs and armpits."
Marie pulled away and went to work on the chicken.
"Bill, you're forgetting us. You have a family, you know."
"I do? That's funny. Some dame just told me that I was losing them."
"Well, maybe she was wrong. Maybe she just loves you. Maybe she hates to see the man she loves go to waste."
"It's just a phase, honey. I'll be all right."
"You're too old for phases," Marie said as she continued at the bird, pulling meat away from skin.
Bill walked into the livingroom to look at Sally. She was sitting on the couch watching Tiny Toons. With the white feathers sticking out

from her head, her red hair looked brighter than usual. Bill smiled at her when she looked at him.

"What Daddy?"

"Nothing, hun. I'll be back."

"You going to a better place?"

Bill smiled, but hurt. He didn't know where he was going, but he needed beer and another bird.

The pet store was on 55th and Bunker. The Fireside was on 54th and Bunker. Bill saw the flashy neon green inviting him in. Burger platters, two dollar taps, and the NCAA tournament. The parking lot was filling up. Suits and ties, muscle shirts and dirty jeans. All classes of working men heading in for drinks. To eat burgers, to watch the game, but mostly to sit together in the dark to be alone.

Bill thought bars were good places. Places where a man could sit with another man and fall apart. Where things were just that, things. And all that really mattered to men that were true men was that eventually they would find their car or truck, or call for a ride so that they could go home.

Inside he was greeted by Martha, the bleach blond divorcee. She was always there, at her place on a black stool at the end of the bar, smoking, laughing, singing along with the jukebox.

"Billy-Boy! Where you been, sweetie?"

"I don't know where I've been, Martha."

Martha patted the stool next to her. "I've missed you, hun. Come and have a seat. Have a drink with Martha."

Bill looked her over and considered it. Martha had been a pretty woman. That's what he'd heard. And he could tell, by her dyed hair and cakey makeup, and by her tight and all too revealing clothes, that like so many others, she was trying to hold on to moments that had passed.

Bill heard his name being called from somewhere behind him. He looked into the bar mirror and could see Jesse's reflection waving.

"Come on, Billy! Grab a glass! You can help me finish off this pitcher!"

Martha reached over the bar and snatched a clean glass from the bartender's hand. She held it out for Bill, but Bill was still looking into the mirror. His face was haggard, his eyes hollow. He lifted his hand to his chin and watched to make sure that the man he was looking at was him. He watched his hand move, white and slow against the darkness of the bar, and everything felt familiar. He watched Martha's reflection until their eyes met in the mirror. He looked away from her then stared into own eyes. They looked like they'd been there before.

"You okay, hun?" Martha asked.

"Yeah, I'm okay. I was just thinking I gotta get to the pet store before it closes."

Bill turned and walked to Jesse.

"She's quite the lady, isn't she?" Jesse said, as he took Bill's glass and filled it.

"She's all lady."

Jesse handed Bill the full glass.

"Killian's...look at it, Bill. It's beautiful."

Bill held the glass to his eyes and peered into it.

"I can hardly see through it. It's so dark."

"It's supposed to be that way."

Bill turned around, still holding the glass to his eyes, and looked through it at Martha.

"Christ! Martha looks like Helen of Troy through this glass!"

Martha turned around and held her glass in the gesture of a toast.

Bill turned toward Jesse. They clinked glasses and drank.

"How's the new life?" Jesse asked.

Bill took another drink. "Not so good, but that's not my biggest problem. Right now I ought to be at the pet store buying my kid a bird."

"Is it her birthday or something?"

"No. She had a bird but I killed it this morning."

Jesse eased his elbows onto the table.

"You did what?"

"Sally was upstairs in her room. The bird wouldn't shut up. I started shaking the goddamned cage and before I knew it, it was dead."

"What did you tell her?"

"I told her that it went to a better place."

"Jeezus, Bill. I bet Marie was pissed."

"Not too bad, but she started in on me about not working, so I decided to leave. I was on my way to the pet store when the glorious neon of the Fireside came calling."

"I know what you mean. I came here right after work. Susan's taking the kids to the library for a story-telling, so I decided to treat myself for a change."

"How's work going for you?" Bill asked.

"What can I say? I stand at a machine all day and press buttons. There's not much to it."

"Yeah, but you make some good bank."

"I guess. I just wish I had the balls to up and quit like you."

"No you don't."

"Sure. Everybody wants to quit and write the great American novel."

"Yeah, but not everybody's wife can support a family on her own."

"That's true."

"Besides, all I'm writing is shit and Marie's getting impatient."

Both men drank some more and watched the big screen. A young woman was racing down a country highway in a glossy black Mitsubishi Eclipse. On the road ahead was a young man hitchhiking and as the car approached, he stepped directly into its path. The woman hit the brakes and the car stopped instantly. She popped her head out of the moon-roof and looked the man up and down. He smiled. She smiled. She nodded toward the passenger side door and he got in. As the new couple drove off into a blue horizon, Mitsubishi reminded viewers that they were not only proud sponsors of the NCAA tournament, but that they were also offering zero down and 2.9% financing to qualified buyers.

"Jesse. What did you want to be?"

Jesse flagged a waitresses and held up the empty pitcher.

"What do you mean?"

"I mean when you were a kid."

"A bus driver."

"A school bus driver?"

"Aw, hell no. A city bus driver. Driving around in that big bus. Making stops, but moving all the time. Watching passengers in the rectangular mirror. Knowing that because of me people were going places. That's what I wanted."

"Think it's too late?"

The waitress set the pitcher down. Bill reached into his pocket to pay.

"What in the hell do you think you're doing? You're a starvin' artist now. You can't pay."

Jesse slapped a twenty onto the table, but the waitress was already walking away.

"Neither of you got it. Our blonde mascot over there said she'd pay for it. You boys better watch it or she's gonna expect one of you to pay her back before the night's over, if you get my drift."

"Good ol' Martha," Bill said.

He and Jesse turned and raised their glasses to her.

"So, do you think it's too late for you to become a bus driver?"

"No. It's never too late. But I got a wife, two kids, a mortgage, car payments. And my wife doesn't work. She takes care of us you know, but she doesn't work. And I got a good job. I don't like it, but it's a good job with good benefits. I'm set, I guess."

"But what about your dream of being a bus driver? Getting all those people to where they want be?"

"I still have it. That's all it is though. A dream. Besides, I got that fucking DWI last year. I can't drive a bus."

"Yeah, I guess you're right. I forgot about that."

"What about you, Billy? What did you want to be?"

Bill looked down into the red beer. An eyelash was floating on the surface. He fished it out with his fingertip and took another drink.

"I don't remember, Jess."

Bill shook his head and looked into the glass again. Jesse leaned back into his chair and sighed.

"Man, you're one depressing sonofabitch. I think I liked it better when you were working all the time and not thinking so much."

"I'm wondering how I killed that bird. I mean I was hungover and feeling like shit, but I never should've killed it."

"So you'll get another bird."

"It's not that. I feel indifferent to everything. To my wife, my kid, to me. It's like I don't know what's real anymore. Like nothing's true."

Jesse topped off their glasses. They sat quietly looking at the big screen. Another commercial. Pete Rose, nodding his head, smiling, talking about the benefits of Dream Home Mortgage company. His hands gesturing to an eight hundred number below him on the screen.

The jukebox had been turned up and Martha was singing along—her voice, a scratchy howl. Bill thought it was The Beatles and that the song was *Strawberry Fields Forever*, but he couldn't be sure. Above everything, Bill could hear a steady flow of laughter rising and falling. Laughter moving from man to man, alternating pitch and tone, but remaining steady.

"Listen Bill, this might not be for me to say, but do you think the booze has anything to do with it? Sue's been talking to Marie and I hear you been drinking pretty early in the day. It's not for me to say, but I am your friend and I do worry about you. Do you think maybe you might need some professional help? It's not a big deal because it seems everybody's getting therapy nowadays."

Bill thought about the bird in the cage. The frantic chirping. The shaking. The flapping wings. The small body thumping against metal bars. Feathers floating. He had heard Sally's bedroom door open, then the bathroom door close, so he ran outside into the alley and threw everything into the dumpster. He was back inside and at the sink washing his hands when Sally came downstairs.

"Where's Sonny?" she had asked.

Bill knelt down to her. He touched the freckles on her nose. He put the feathers in her hair. She smiled at him then danced away into the livingroom. *To a better place*, Bill thought over and over as he opened the refrigerator for V-8 juice and beer.

"A professional would say I'm depressed because of drinking. That drinking's part of the problem I'm having fulfilling my roles. They'd tag all sorts of terms onto me. But the truth is that it's my life. I quit my job and Marie doesn't understand because I don't understand. All I'm sure of is that I'm tired, Jesse, and even though I feel indifferent, it feels right."

"Okay. How much have you had to drink today?"

"Jess. My life was a lie. And I can't live a lie."

"Everybody's got lies, Bill."

"Then where's the truth? Is it hidden? Maybe it's in the dark, not the light."

Bill stopped. Jesse topped off their glasses again.

"Bill, you're talking crazy, like my fucking wife. What are you trying to get at? The Subconscious or something?"

"Something like that."

"So you killed a bird and quit your job because killing and quitting are things you really want to do."

"Okay, I'm not making sense. I'll shut up."

"No, Billy! Keep going. I'm just a bit slow when it comes to this shit. I'm trying like hell to understand."

"I think part of the reason I drink is because I'm restless. Like I'm looking for something. And I know the answer isn't in drinking, but it gives me a filter to run things through. I think sometimes I can find the truth better when I'm in the dark."

"If you're looking for truth, why the bar? Why not at home with your family? We're big boys now. Do you realize this? We're supposed to be taking care of the family and getting things done."

"Are we? Or is that what we're trained to do? To be good fathers and husbands. To provide. And is any of that shit true?"

"I hope to hell it is, since that's the way I'm living."

"Listen Jesse, I don't mean to get down on anybody's way of life. What I'm interested in is finding the truth."

"The truth about what?"

"The truth about all of this. Like being here, talking like this. It's the only time we can talk like this. In here, in the dark of the bar. We can't talk like this at home, can we?"

"No, not around the kids, anyway. But I think you're thinking about it too much. Why can't we just sit and drink like we used to?"

They raised their glasses and Jesse made a toast.

"Here's to staying in the dark, like me. To hell with thinking and to hell with the truth. All I know is that this beer tastes good, Martha can't sing, and I'm getting drunk."

"You have it there, my friend. And maybe that's the only way to find it."

"Or maybe, Billy-boy, there's nothing to find."

Bill sat back and watched a waitress wearing tight black shorts and a wide smile slip through drunk and drinking bodies with a food platter high above her head in one hand and two pitchers of beer in the other. He envied her balance.

"You gonna be okay, Bill?"
"I think so."
"Wanna get another pitcher?"
"No, I gotta get going."
"To a better place, right?" Jesse laughed.
"Nope. Just to the pet store."
Bill stood and felt the good rush of blood and alcohol washing his brain. As he walked to the door, Martha stood and came to him.
"Not even a thank you?" She cooed.
Bill leaned into her and they hugged. He could feel her soft bulkiness under the tight clothes.
"Thanks for the beer, Martha."
"Where are you going? Maybe we could do something?"
"Nope. Afraid not. I gotta buy a bird."

Bill looked up the street toward the pet store. He could see its yellow sign hanging above the sidewalk. Men and women who had been working late were hustling around him. Some of them on phones, some of them nearly running, none of them smiling.
The store's lights were on, but the door was locked. A young looking man and a younger looking woman were at the counter removing register tapes and putting money into a deposit bag. Bill checked his watch. It was twelve after six. He stood at the window and stared inside. He could see the BirdWall on the left side of the store. Cages and cages of birds. Hundreds of them safe under the fluorescent glow of overhead lights. Bill rapped on the window.
"Hey! Can I get in for a minute!"
The young man and young woman looked at each other. When the man nodded toward the door, the woman came over and pointed to the hours sign hanging in the window.
"We closed at six. We open at nine tomorrow."

"I know that, but…well, it's just my little girl is very sick and she really wants a bird. A certain type of bird. If you could just let me in for a minute it would really help me out."

The woman looked him over. Bill could see his reflection in the window. Unshaven. Messy hair. Hollow eyes. He was thin and pale and looking very much older than 35.

The woman stepped away from the window and said something to the man. The man stopped his work at the counter then came over to the girl. Both of them stood at the window looking at Bill. He felt like he was on display. He could see transparent people and cars crossing behind him. Shapes moving all around in the window glass.

The man came to the door and poked his head out. "Sir, we're closed for the night, but if you know exactly what you need I can let you in for a few minutes."

"I need a white bird. Like those over on the wall. That's what I need."

"Okay, but could I see some identification? For security purposes, you understand."

"Sure, sure. Here's my license."

Bill handed him the card. The picture didn't look anything like him anymore. It had been summer when the picture was taken. His face was clean, tan. His hair was cut short and had been lightened by the sun. He, Marie, and Sally had been spending their weekends at the cottage on Grand Lake. The cottage that Sally called the fun house. The one she knew as her first home.

He remembered being at lakeside most nights. Sitting in his shorts. Warmed by a nightcap, the fire, and the sight of Marie and Sally making S'mores. The pop-crackling of jumping flames. The crickets. The water soft against the shore. Everything was different now and Bill wondered what was real.

The man returned the license then spoke to the woman as he opened the door.

"Steffie, do you want me to go with him?"

The woman rolled her eyes at this, then smiled at Bill. She pounded her fist into her palm for effect.

"No James, I think I can handle this one."

Bill looked at Steffie. She had a deep-dimpled smile and wild green eyes. Her hair was light brown, her nose and cheeks were splashed with freckles. He thought of Sally at home eating supper in the livingroom without her Daddy and he wondered how everything came to be.

"I really appreciate this. Not many stores would do this for a customer."

"I know how it is when a kid gets sick. You want to do whatever it takes to make them happy."

Steffie walked by Bill's side to the bird wall. He could smell her.

"Is that you that smells like vanilla?"

She stopped before a cage of white birds and took a ring of keys out of her pocket. Her face turned red as she fumbled for the right one.

"My son bought if for me. He says it makes me smell like candy."

"Son? You can't be old enough to have children."

"I have two boys. Got started young in the kid department, I guess."

Bill remembered the first year with Marie. Both of them young and struggling through winter, living in the small cottage on Grand Lake, trying to save as much money as they could so that they could move into a real home come summer time. A large two story with an attached two-car-garage and a big green backyard. A new home to go with his new family.

And Bill felt, always, an urgency to move ahead, to provide, to get up and off to work early and to come home late six days a week. It was a strange, hard feeling and he thought that it stemmed from the responsibility of new life—his daughter, Sally. She was fresh and newborn and restless, and although the sight, sound, and feel of her made him uneasy at times, she overwhelmed him with purpose and warmth.

He remembered then, Marie getting out of bed all those nights to comfort Sally. Most nights it was the absence of Marie's warmth that would wake him. He would rise then, awake with his urgency, and follow their sounds into the livingroom. Rocking in the chair by the fire, Marie talked to Sally in whispers.

"It's too cold in this tiny shack, isn't it honey? That's why you're upset, isn't it? Daddy's fire has gone out."

So Bill would head outside in his pajamas to carry in another armload of wood. He'd stay up then, because there was no use in going back to bed when he had to be up in a few hours. He'd make coffee then sit near the fire stirring the coals, adding more wood, watching Marie's eyelids rise and fall. Finally, when Sally was asleep, he'd take her and watch Marie shuffle off to bed. Bill would sit by the fire then, holding his daughter, wondering at her smallness and how it made him feel so big.

Steffie rattled the keys and wings flapped. Feathers and bird seed jumped out of the cage. Bill watched Steffie as she reached in and cradled a bird in her hands.

"Did he look like this?"

"Yeah, but I don't know if it was a he."

"How old's your daughter."

"She'll be seven in December."

"Really? What day? My youngest's birthday is in December. He'll be six."

"Sally was born on the 13th."

"David was born on the sixth! Winter babies! Maybe they'll grow up and get married!"

Bill felt a ball in his throat, but managed to smile. He'd never thought that far ahead before.

"Anyway," Steffie said, "If you couldn't tell what it was then I don't think she'll notice a difference."

"I hope you're right."

"What was it's name?"

"Sonny."

She held the bird up to Bill's face. Bill tilted his head to get a better look. The bird did the same.

"Sonny, meet Dad."

Bill remembered the cage.

"You know what? I don't know if I have enough money for a cage. With all the running I've been doing today I forgot to bring a cage."

"That's okay. We can work something out. Let me and Sonny go talk to James and I'll meet you up front in a few minutes."

Bill walked past the wall of birds and he could feel them watching him. Blue ones, yellow ones, some chirping, some huddled together in silence with puffed feathers on perches.

Bill leaned against the counter and looked outside. The sun was down. The sky was a thick, dark blue. Streetlights were on. People on the sidewalks were younger now. Couples holding hands, walking side by side, heading to movies, clubs, or parties. Bill could see his reflection again, but ignored it. Instead, he watched Steffie coming up the aisle behind him. She had a cloth draped over a cage.

"Here he is!" she chimed. "And I talked to James. He said that if you can't pay now that I'm supposed to take your name and number. But if you don't come in to pay in a couple of days we'll send the bird police after you."

Steffie took out a receipt book.

"Do you need my license?" He asked.

"No, I trust you."

"William Simms. 1427 Buck Hill Lane, Berry Grove, Minnesota, 55012. My number is 651-632-1566."

"Do you have an alternate number you can be reached at? Like a work number, or a cell phone number?

"No, I don't."

Steffie separated the copies and handed him one.

"That's okay, that's enough information. You better be on your way. You've got a little girl waiting, and I've got to get back there and help James. The door locks automatically when you leave."

Bill took the cage. He looked at Steffie, but she was already turned away heading toward the back of the store. He knew that if he wanted to he could take anything. Birds, fish, plastic hamster wheels. He watched Steffie walk and thought maybe he should have told her the truth.

Outside it was cold. The air was still, but biting. As Bill walked, he searched the stars hoping to find something he knew. The Big Dipper, the North Star, the Moon. But nothing came together. The stars, some of them shimmering bluish-white, were familiar because he had watched them drift through different skies all his life, but he had forgotten their names. He was certain he had known them once, on one of those nights at the cottage when Sally was three or four. She was on his lap staring into the sky through a pair of binoculars that were too heavy for her to hold on her own and Bill did his best to help her, steadying her hands and naming the stars, but Sally was only interested in the moon.

"What's the moon, Daddy?"

"It's a dead star."

"But it's there. I can see it."

"It is, isn't it?"

Sally nodded then let go of the binoculars. Bill put them to his eyes and stared at the moon. Its pockmarked surface was orangishwhite and he thought for a moment that maybe it was true what he had heard as a kid, that the moon was made of cheese.

"Is it really dead?" Sally asked.

Hearing her say it, *"Is it really dead?"*, had sent cold up the back of his neck.

"No Sally, I was wrong. Daddy was thinking of something else. The moon is alive. It's just old. I can see it right there myself."

He held her tight till the cold went away.

Bill could feel the cold air creeping through him. The bird ruffled its feathers and he imagined that it too must be cold. Even though Steffie had placed a cloth over the cage, Bill wasn't taking any chances. He took off his coat, draped it over the cage and carried the bird against his chest.

When he got back to the Fireside parking lot, he noticed that he had been parked in. The front end of a red Ford pickup was against his rear bumper. Bill opened his car, started it, then buckled the bird cage into the backseat. He took a pen out of the glove box and went around to the back of the truck. He bent down to one knee and scribbled the plate number onto the palm of his hand.

The Fireside door opened and for a moment the inside of the bar was let out. The music and laughter, the shouting and the clinking of glasses. Bill stayed behind the truck, listening. He could hear a man at the door yelling inside to another man.

"Come on Jerry! We ain't got all night! Besides, I told Eddie we'd be there already!"

Bill could hear another man yelling too, but couldn't understand him because the musical drunkenness of the bar was distorting the words.

Bill stood up and watched the man at the door. He wondered if it might be Jesse and he wanted to call out, but he held silent instead. The man was a shadow outlined in neon green. He wobbled and yelled until the other man joined him. Then they stood in the doorway, arguing over who would drive. Finally, the door was slammed and the men staggered into the dark. Their bodies had disappeared but Bill could hear their heavy voices and shuffling feet coming near.

"Hey Tom! There's somebody by your truck! Hey you! What are you doing there!"

This was what it was like from the outside, Bill thought. When the truth was caught between the light of the bar and the stars. He stepped out from behind the truck and moved toward the Fireside. He could no longer hear the men, their feet and voices, or the engine of his own car, because he was thinking of Sally and the dead bird and doubting that this new bird would make any difference at all.

He moved quickly hoping that Jesse or Martha was still there and that the drunks wouldn't follow him, but out of the darkness they came and suddenly he was being pushed against the truck. He felt the sideview mirror give way under his back and heard a metallic pop.

"What the hell are you doing messing around by my truck?"

"I'm sorry, but that's my car there, and I want to get out."

"Then what are you doing breaking my mirror?"

"I'm sorry, but you pushed me into it. Maybe it just got bumped out of place."

"What were you trying to do? Steal it?"

"No. I was just writing your plate number down. I was gonna head back inside and see if I could find you, but since you're here I guess you saved me a trip."

The man stepped forward and Bill could sense the other man circling around from behind. He turned his body sideways so that he could find both of them in the dark.

"What's this guy want, Tom?"

Both men were short and stocky. By their size and shape, and the sound of their voices, Bill thought they could be twins.

"I don't know, Jerry, but I think he's trying to fuck with me! You fuckin' with me, mister?"

"Listen, I'm sorry. My kid's sick and I just want to go home. Could you please move your truck?"

Jerry, the man at the back of the truck, piped up. "I never even seen this guy in the bar. I think he's lyin'! He's probably a just goddamned thief!"

Tom, the man who had started it all, steadied himself against the cab. "Yeah, I never seen him neither. What are you tryin' to pull here, buddy?"

"Listen. I was in the bar earlier, but then I walked down to the pet store to get a bird for my kid because she's sick and…"

"He's a liar!" Jerry yelled as he moved closer. "Look at him, Tom! He ain't got no coat on! Why would he be out walking in the cold without a goddamned coat!"

Bill felt hot. His hand balled into a fist around the ink pen.

"That's my car right there, you assholes! The one parked in! I don't have my coat on because it's in the car keeping the bird warm!"

They laughed at him and one of them shouted, "Ain't it sweet? A bird lover!"

Bill felt a hand on his shoulder.

"Take your hand off me!"

It was getting hard to tell which man was which. Both of them were at him now, pushing. Bill felt a hand near his face.

"He's a pretty little birdie, ain't he?"

"Let's pluck him and stuff him!"

Bill could see the moon behind the men. It was a thin orange wedge. He wondered why he hadn't noticed it earlier. Where had it come from, and what was it made of?

"Is it really dead?"

"No Sally, I was wrong. Daddy was thinking of something else."

Then it came. A heavy thump in the gut. All air and sense wheezed out of Bill's body as he doubled over, gasping. He could hear the men laughing, threatening again to stuff him like a bird.

He sucked in as much of the night as he could, held the pen tight and began swinging it at their legs. Swinging and missing, swinging and missing, until finally he connected just above a knee. He could tell, as the howling trailed off behind the truck, that it was Jerry.

Bill stood up and tried to get more air. As Tom stepped forward and started punching, Bill reached up with the pen. He shoved it against Tom's neck as hard as he could without sticking it in.

"Move your fucking truck right now!"

The Fireside door opened and another man was approaching. Bill imagined he was done for. That the three of them would take him down with fists and kicks, maybe a tire-iron too. He imagined himself on his back trying to breathe, all the while searching the sky and thinking of the bird in the idling car. How long would it last there under the coat and buckled in?

He felt the third man at his back so he whirled around with the pen in both hands high above his head.

"Billy! Bill! It's me!"

He could barely make out the body in the dark, but as air filled up his lungs and gave him sense again he could feel that it was Jesse.

"What the hell are you doing?" Jesse asked.

"These guys parked me in!"

"Is that a knife? Jesus! Put that down!"

Jesse's voice sounded good in the dark. Bill lowered the pen and backed away. The man named Tom reached into his pocket and took out his keys. He opened his door and climbed into the truck.

"I don't know who you guys are, but you ought to have your goddamned heads examined!"

Jerry, the passenger, was already inside the truck, weeping.

Jesse and Bill watched the truck back out of the driveway then roar off down the road.

"Bill, what are you doing?"

"I don't know."

"You're scaring the shit out of me. What was that in your hand?"
"A pen. I was just writing down their fucking plate number."
"Are you nuts? People get killed because of shit like that."
"For writing down numbers?"
"No, for trying to take on two guys with an ink pen!"
"They weren't two guys. That was Tom and Jerry."

Bill handed Jesse the pen. He felt alive and couldn't help smiling as he got into his car. It was warm inside and Bill remembered the bird. He reached over the seat and tapped the cage. The bird ruffled its feathers and Bill was relieved. He backed out onto the road then looked over to wave at Jesse but it was too dark and Jesse couldn't see him.

The streets were bright. The sky looked bigger than usual. Hours had passed but Bill felt like he'd been gone for days. He remembered waking with a hangover to the sound of a chirping bird. He remembered shaking the cage, killing the bird, and lying. Lying to Sally. Lying to Marie. Lying to everyone. He remembered that the truth was that it was March and it was cold. The truth was that April and May would have to pass before Bill and Marie could take Sally out to the cottage. By then, it would be warm enough for them to live there for a week or two. And Bill thought that when the time came it would be good because it would be like starting over.

When he pulled into the driveway, the lights were on. He could see Marie in the livingroom. She was on the sofa reading the newspaper. She'd be angry, but she wouldn't say anything because he would have the bird. It was an offering. A way of trying to right the wrong. Bill shut off the headlights and sat in the car. He watched Marie stand and look outside into the dark. She was leaning over the sofa with her hands cupping the sides of her eyes like binoculars.

Bill shut off the car and opened the door. He reached into the backseat and unbuckled the bird. He thought of taking his coat off the cage but left it on in hopes of keeping things quiet. He rattled the cage as he pulled it out of the car and the bird started chirping. Bill thought of how careful he must be.

He closed the car door and carried the bird to the door. Marie was waiting, standing firm with her arms crossed, but when she saw the cage and heard the bird she began to smile. Bill handed her the cage, kissed her nose, and was happy to be home.

0-595-22424-5